7/92

TO TAME A LAND

TO TAME
A LAND

LOUIS L'AMOUR

BANTAM BOOKS
TORONTO • NEW YORK • LONDON • SYDNEY • AUCKLAND

All characters in this book are fictional,
and any resemblance to persons, living or dead,
is purely coincidental.

TO TAME A LAND

*A Bantam Book / published by arrangement with
the Author*

PRINTING HISTORY

Bantam edition / January 1984

The Louis L'Amour Collection / January 1987

*If you would be interested in receiving bookends for The Louis
L'Amour Collection, please write to this address for information:*

The Louis L'Amour Collection
Bantam Books
P.O. Box 956
Hicksville, New York 11802

ISBN 0-553-06295-6

Published simultaneously in the United States and Canada

*Bantam Books are published by Bantam Books, Inc. Its trademark,
consisting of the words "Bantam Books" and the portrayal of a
rooster, is Registered in U.S. Patent and Trademark Office and in
other countries. Marca Registrada. Bantam Books, Inc., 666 Fifth
Avenue, New York, New York 10103.*

PRINTED IN THE UNITED STATES OF AMERICA

0   9   8   7   6   5   4   3   2   1

TO TAME A LAND

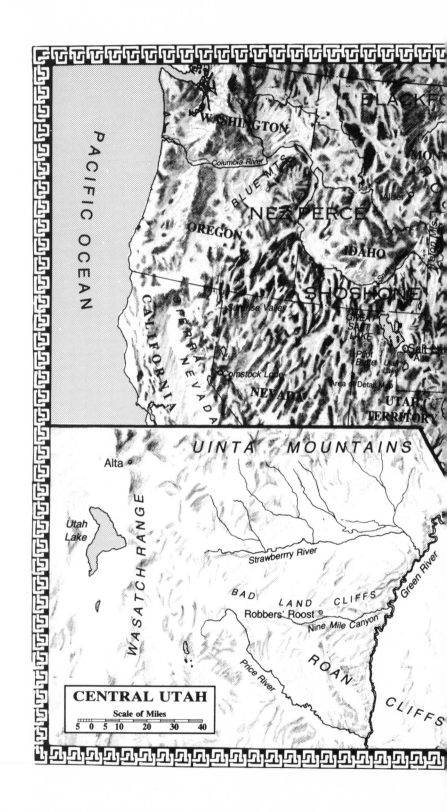

PACIFIC OCEAN

WASHINGTON

Columbia River

BLUE MTS.

OREGON

NEZ PERCE

IDAHO

BLACKF

MON

Weiser

Sn

SHOSHONE

CALIFORNIA

SIERRA NEVADA

Sunrise Valley

GREAT
SALT
LAKE

Pilot
Butte

Salt
Lake

Salt
City

Comstock Lode

NEVADA

Area of Detail Map

UTAH
TERRITORY

UINTA MOUNTAINS

Alta

WASATCH RANGE

Utah
Lake

Strawberry River

BAD   LAND   CLIFFS

Robbers' Roost

Nine Mile Canyon

Green River

Price River

ROAN

CLIFFS

CENTRAL UTAH

Scale of Miles

5 0 5 10   20   30   40

WESTERN U.S.

Scale of Miles

0   50   100   150   200   250

NORTH DAKOTA

MINNESOTA

WISCONSIN

Mississippi River

SOUTH DAKOTA

NG

CHEYENNE

SIOUX

IOWA

Platte River

NEBRASKA

Missouri River

Cheyenne

Denver

Kansas City

St. Louis

KANSAS

OSAGE

MISOURRI

ORADO

Dodge

Wichita

Cimarron River

Old Spanish Trail

North Canadian River

KIOWA

Canadian River

INDIAN TERRITORY

ARKANSAS

Santa Fe

Tascosa

HE

EXICO

Red River

TORY

COMANCHE

Marshall

TEXAS

o Grande

San Antonio

Uvalde

Gulf of Mexico

Map by Alan McKnight

ONE

It was Indian country, and when our wheel busted, none of them would stop. They just rolled on by and left us setting there, my pap and me.

Me, I was pushing a tall twelve by then and could cuss 'most as good as Pap, and we both done some cussin' then.

Bagley, the one Pap helped down to Ash Hollow that time, he got mighty red around the ears, but he kept his wagon rollin'.

Most folks, those days, were mighty helpful, but this outfit sort of set their way by the captain. He was Big Jack McGarry.

When the wheel busted, somebody called out and we swung back. Big Jack had no liking for Pap because Pap never took nothing off him, and because Pap had the first look-in with Mary Tatum, which Big Jack couldn't abide.

He swung that fine black horse of his back and he set there looking at us. We had turned to and were getting that wheel off, fixing to get it repaired if we could.

"Sorry, Tyler. You know what I said. This is Indian country. Goin' through here, we keep rollin' no matter what. We'll wait a spell at the springs, though. You can catch us there."

Then he turned his horse and rode off, and nobody else in the wagons said by word or look that they even seen us setting there.

1

Pap, he didn't waste no more time. He looked after them, his face kind of drawn down and gray like, and then he turned to me and he said, "Son, I don't mind for myself. It's you I'm thinkin' of. But maybe it'll be all right. You take that there gun, and you set up high and watch sharp."

So that was the way it was, and Pap aworking to fix that wheel so we could go on. He was a good man at such things, and he had built many a wagon in his day, and had done some fine cabinetwork, too.

He worked steady and I kept my eyes open, but there was mighty little to see. It was a long rolling grass plain wherever a body looked. Here and there was draws, but I couldn't see into them. The wind stirred that tall grass, bending it over in long rolls, the way the sea must look, and it was green-gray and then silver in the changing light and wind. Overhead the sky was wide and pale blue, with just a few lazy clouds adrifting.

We had us a good Conestoga wagon and six head of cattle, good big oxen, to haul it. We had two horses and two saddles, and inside the wagon was Pap's tools, our grub, bedding, and a few odds and ends like Ma's picture, which Pap kept by him, no matter what.

Pap had swapped for a couple of Joslyn breech-loading carbines before we left Kansas, and we each had us a handgun, Shawk & McLanahan six-shooters, caliber .36, and good guns, too.

Like McGarry said, this was Indian country. Not two weeks ago the Indians had hit a wagon train, smaller than ours, killing four men and a woman. They hit it again a few miles west, and they killed two more men.

Ours was a big train, well armed and all, but Big Jack, I seen the look in his eyes when he sat there watching Pap aworking. He was just figuring to himself that he wouldn't have to worry any more about Pap, and by the time the wagons got to Californy he'd be married up with Mary Tatum. Her and all that silver her old man carried in the big box under his wagon.

When it was almost dark, Pap called to me. "Son, come on

2

down. You ride your horse, scout around a little. If the wagons get to stop at the springs, we'll catch 'em."

But cattle don't make no speed with a heavy wagon. Their feet spread wide on turf and they pull better, day in, day out, than any mule or horse, but they can't be called fast.

Night came, and we set a course by the stars, and we rolled on west all through the night. When the first gray light was in the sky, we saw the gleam on the water. Least, I saw it. Pap, he was still too far back.

I seen the water where the pool was, and the cottonwood leaves, but no white wagon covers, no horses, and no breakfast fires acooking.

When the wagon came up I saw Pap looking and looking like he couldn't believe it, and I seen his Adam's apple swallow, and I said, "Pap, they've gone on. They left us."

"Yes," he said. "I reckon that's so."

We both knew we had to stop. Cattle can stand so much, and these had a tough night and day behind them. "We'll water up, son," Pap said. "Then we'll pull into a draw and rest a while."

So that was how it was, only when we got to the springs we saw the wagons had not stopped there. Big Jack McGarry had taken no chances. He pulled them right on by, and nobody to know he'd promised to wait for us there. Nobody but him and us.

We watered up and then we pulled out. Maybe three miles farther on we found a draw with some brush and we pulled into it for a rest. Pap unyoked the oxen and let them eat buffalo grass. He taken his Joslyn up on the ridge and bellied down in the grass.

Me, I went to sleep under the wagon, and maybe I'd been asleep an hour when I felt someone nudge me, and it was Pap.

"Here they come, boy. You get on your horse and take out." He was down on one knee near me. "Maybe if you hold to low ground you can make it safe."

"I ain't agoin' without you."

3

"Son, you go now. One can make it. Two can't. You take Old Blue. He's the fastest."

"You come with me."

"No, this here is all we got, boy. I'll stay by it. Maybe they'll take what sugar we got, and go."

"I'll stay, too."

"No!" Pap rarely spoke hard to me after Ma died, but he spoke sharp and stern now, and it wasn't in me to dispute him. So I loosed the reins and swung into the saddle.

Pap passed me up a sackful of cartridges and such, then caught my arm. There were tears in his eyes. "Luck, boy. Luck. Remember your ma."

Then he slapped Old Blue on the rump and Old Blue went off up the draw. Me, I was in no mind to leave him, so when we rounded a little bend I put Blue up the bank and circled back.

I heard a rifle shot and saw dust kick near the wagon, then a whole volley of shots. Along with the rest I heard the sharp hard sound of Pap's Joslyn carbine.

Tying Blue among some brush in a low place, I grabbed my Joslyn and went back, keeping low down.

Maybe a dozen Indians were out there, and Pap's one shot had counted, for I saw a free horse running off. As I looked the Indians began to circle, and Pap fired again. An Indian grabbed at his horse's mane and almost slipped off.

The sun was out and it was hot. I could smell the hot, dusty grass and feel the sun on my back, and my hands were sweaty, but I waited.

Boy though I was, and Pap no Indian fighter, I knew what I had to do. Night after night I'd sat by the fire and heard talk of Indian fights and such-like from the mountain men we met, and a couple of others who had been over this trail before us. I soaked it up, and I knew there was a time for waiting and a time for shooting.

Pap was doing right good. He downed a horse and the Indians pulled off and away. I lay quiet, having a good view of

4

the whole shindig, me being no more than a hundred and fifty yards off.

Sudden-like, I saw the grass move. They were crawling up now. Did Pap see them?

No, he couldn't see them from where he lay, but he had guessed that was what they would do, for I saw him worm out from behind the wheel where he'd been shooting and ease off into some rocks not far from the wagon. They were coming on and right soon I could see four of the Indians.

Pap waited. I give him that. He was no Indian fighter, just a good wheelwright and cabinetmaker, but he was smart. Suddenly he came up with his carbine and fired quick. I saw an Indian jerk back with a busted shoulder. Then two of them ran forward. Pap fired and missed, and fired again and hit.

And then I heard a whisper in the grass and saw four Indians walking their horses careful behind him. Behind him and right below me. They weren't thirty yards off from me, at point-blank range.

This here was what I'd waited for. My mouth so dry I couldn't spit or swallow, I ups with my Joslyn. I took steady aim the way I'd been taught, drew a deep breath and let it out easy, and then I squeezed her off. The rifle jumped in my hands, and that first Indian let out a grunt and went off his horse and into the grass. I'd shot him right through the skull.

Pap turned quick, fired once, then swung back as I shot again.

My second shot took an Indian right through the spine, and the other two went to hellin' away from there.

My shooting had caught them flat-footed, as the fellow says. They'd figured the man at the wagon was the only one, and now I'd killed me two Indians, and all in less than a minute.

Another shot, and I turned quick.

Two Indians had rushed Pap and now they were fighting with him. At the same moment the two I'd run off circled back. I shot and missed, too excited, and then I saw Pap go down

5

and saw a knife rise and fall, and I knew it was too late to do anything for Pap.

I hustled for Old Blue, jumped into the saddle, and rode out of there.

But I didn't head for no settlement, or try to catch up with the train. That wagon was ours, and the stuff in it was ours. I circled around, walked my horse a couple of miles in a creek, then brought him out of the water onto rock and cut back over the hills.

It was full dark when I got back there. All was quiet. There was no fire, nothing.

I studied about it some, then decided those Indians would never figure on me to come back, and once they'd taken what they wanted from the wagon, they'd not stay around. So I went down, taking it easy. Finally, when Old Blue began to get nervous, I tied him to a bush and went on alone.

When I got close I could smell the burned wood. The wagon had been set on fire, but it was still there.

I crawled up closer, and I found Pap. He'd been shot through, then stabbed. And they'd scalped him.

Using a match, I hunted through the wagon. They'd looted it, throwing stuff around, taking most of what they could use. I knew where Pap had kept the forty dollars in gold he had, and with my knife point I dug it out of a crack in the wood Pap had puttied over.

They'd set fire to the wagon, all right, but only the cover had burned. The hoops were some charred, and the sideboards, but most of the stuff was intact. Pap's tool chest had been busted open, and most of the sharp tools were gone. The chisels and like that.

There was a few cents change in Pap's pocket, and I took it. He'd be wanting me to have it.

Then I got the shovel and dug out a grave for him on the hill, and there I toted his body and buried him, crying all the time like a durned girl-baby. Me, who bragged it up that I never shed no tears.

On the grave I piled some rocks and on a piece of board I burned out Pap's name with a hot iron. Then I rustled around amongst what was left to see what I could find.

There was little enough, but I found Ma's picture. Miracle was, it hadn't burned. But it was stuck down in the Bible and only the edges of the leaves had charred a mite, and the cover. I put Ma's picture in my pocket and went back to Old Blue.

The cattle were gone. They'd drove them off and somewhere now they were eating real big.

Eating . . . eating too much and maybe sleeping. Eating too much and in their own country, and they wouldn't be keeping a guard, maybe.

The nearest water was where they would head for, and the nearest water was the springs. I got up on Old Blue and started walking him back.

Maybe I was just a fool kid, but those Indians had killed Pap and stolen our cattle. I was going to get me an Indian.

One more, anyway.

TWO

The night smelled good. There were a million stars in the sky, looked like, and I could feel the soft wind over the grass. And on that wind I smelled smoke; wood smoke, with some smell of buffalo chips, too.

Old Blue seemed to know what I was about. He walked real light and easy on the grass, his ears pricked up. He could smell the smoke, and from the uneasy feel of him between my knees, I knew he could smell Indian.

After a while I got down and tied Old Blue. Then I crept along, all bent over, and got up close.

They had a fire that was almost dead, and I could see their horses off to one side. They were all asleep, expecting nothing. I could see four oxen still standing, so they had only eaten two, or most of two.

Take white men a week to eat an ox, but not Indians. They gorged themselves one day, starved the next; that was the way of it. Well, one or more had eaten all he was ever going to.

First off I crawled around to where their ponies were. Working up close through the grass, I got up and walked casual-like among them. Maybe because of that, maybe because I was just a boy, they didn't fret much until I had my hand on a tie rope. Then one of them blew loud through his nostrils.

And when he done that, I slashed the picket ropes with my

9

pocket knife, first one, then another. Then I yelled and two of the horses done what I'd hoped. They ran full tilt into that Indian camp. I held my fire until I saw Indians scrambling up, and then I shot.

I shot three times as fast as I could trigger that Joslyn. Then I hauled out my old Shawk & McLanahan .36 and, running up close, I fired three times more.

Two Indians were down, one of them holding his belly. Another was staggering with a bullet through his leg. But that was enough. I turned and got out of there almighty fast. When I was a distance away, I circled around to Old Blue.

Once in the saddle, I headed off across country. Twice I came up to Indian ponies from the bunch I'd stampeded and started them moving again.

All night I rode on, heading west along the track of the wagons. Come day, I found a place high on a hill where there was a sort of hollow. I picketed Old Blue and stretched out on my back.

The sun woke me up, shining right in my face. I got up on Old Blue again and headed west. Next day I killed a buffalo calf. Here and there I found some wild onions, and I ate the buffalo meat without salt.

It was like that for a week. Finally I got so I rode mostly at night, using the stars to travel by, as Pap had shown me. Indians don't travel by night much, and they don't like night fighting, so it was safer. By day I'd hole up and keep out of sight. Twice I saw Indians, but not up close, and none of them saw me.

Twice I found burned wagons, but they were old fires of wagons burned long ago.

I rode west. I saw the grass plains left behind and high mountains roll up, and sometimes I saw buffalo, and lots of antelope. I was sparing of my ammunition, and I never tried any long shots. Usually I'd work in close and try to cut out a buffalo calf. The old cows were mighty fractious, and sometimes I'd kill one of them, usually with the pistol, at close range.

But there was meat, and there were always onions. Once I caught me a mess of fish and fried them in buffalo fat for my meal.

There were beaver streams, and more and more trees on the mountains, and the country became rougher.

It was two weeks before I caught up with the wagon train, even though I could travel faster than they. Two weeks because I'd taken time out to hunt grub, and because they had a good two-day start on me. Also, I was riding mighty careful. I didn't want my hair hanging in no Arapaho wickiup.

When at last I saw the wagon train it was in South Pass. Old Blue carried me down out of the hills and I took him at a lope across the grassy valley that lies between the Sweetwater Mountains and the Wind River Range.

The wagons stretched out, white and long, the horsemen rode alongside, and a lump came up in my throat when I thought of Pap and his wagon. He could have been here, too, if they'd stopped to wait. Right then I hated every one of them, but most of all I hated Big Jack McGarry.

It was Bagley I saw first. His face went kind of white when he saw me. "Rye!" he said. "Where's your Pap?"

Wagons drew up and several riders started toward me. McGarry started back from the head of the wagon train.

"He's dead," I told them, tears starting into my eyes. "He's dead, and you all killed him. You could have waited."

"Waited? Where?" Bagley was angry. "Risk our families? What you talkin' of, boy?"

"McGarry said you'd wait at the springs. He told Pap that. We got to the springs right quick, and you all didn't even stop."

There was a slim, wiry man in buckskins setting a black horse there, and he looked at me. "Boy, are you sure Big Jack promised to wait at the springs?"

"I'm damn sure!"

Big Jack came up then and pushed his horse through the

circle. "Here! What's this? You're holdin' up the . . . Oh, it's you."

You didn't need to look close to see he wasn't happy to see me. His face showed mighty plain that he had never expected us to come through . . . and only one of us had.

The slim man in buckskins looked over at Big Jack. "Jack, the boy says you told his pap you'd wait at the springs."

"He lies!" McGarry said angrily. "The boy lies. I told him nothing of the kind."

"You did so." I put my hand on my Shawk & McLanahan. "You say I lie and I'll shoot you sure."

The man in the buckskins shook his head at me. "Sit quiet, boy. We'll get the straight of this." He turned back to McGarry. "I never did understand why we passed up the sweetest water in a hundred miles. It was early to stop, but with that wagon left behind . . . ?"

"I told him no such thing! What would I do that for?"

"Because Pap wasn't afeared of you. And because you were shinin' up to Mary Tatum."

That man hated me. I could see it in his hard little eyes. "Boy, you shet that mouth! You shet up or I'll blister your hide!"

"You'll blister no hides, McGarry. You've a question or two to answer." The man in buckskins turned and looked at Mary Tatum. "Ma'am, I reckon we all know McGarry's been wantin' to court you. You been talkin' with him some. Did you set out with him so much when Tyler was with us?"

Mary was a right pretty girl and she had spunk. I knowed Pap set a sight of store by her, and he had asked me once what I'd think of her as a mother. I told him that seeing as how my own ma was buried back East, there was nobody I'd like better.

Now she lifted her chin and said quietly, "I was thinking a lot about Mr. Tyler. He was a good man and an honest man. I believe he was in love with me."

"I know he was," I said.

She looked at me, her gray eyes wide and full. Then she said quietly, "I am a single girl and I want a husband. I hoped to marry Ralph Tyler. I have never even considered marrying Jack McGarry, and will not now."

McGarry's face went red, then white. He started to speak.

The man in buckskins interrupted. "We don't know the straight of this, and I reckon we'll never know exactly. If you told him we'd wait at the springs, we should have waited. We should have stopped there, anyway. I wondered why we didn't. I think you're guilty."

I expected McGarry to grab for his gun, but he didn't. There was something about that slender man that didn't look very safe.

A solidly built man in a black coat and flat black hat spoke up. "We'll be having an election. We'll be wanting a new captain."

Big Jack McGarry looked over at me and there was nothing nice in his eyes. He looked mighty mean.

Mary Tatum saw it, and she walked over to my horse. "Rye," she said gently, "I'm very sorry about Ralph. Will you ride with us now?"

"No, ma'am," I said, "but I thank you. I don't figure to stay with this outfit." I looked over at Bagley. "There's some folks here won't feel right as long as I'm about."

"But, Rye, you're only a boy!" she protested.

"I killed me three Indians," I said. "I've come across the plains these last days all by myself. I'll go on by myself."

She smiled at me. "All right, Rye, but will you eat with us this night?"

"Yes, ma'am. I'll be obliged."

It was mighty good, setting up to a civilized meal again. Mary Tatum was a wonderful cook, and she even managed some cookies, and most of them she gave to me. Night came, and when I got my buffalo robe she brought me blankets from her own wagon.

"Ma'am," I said, "I'd have liked it, having you for a ma."

She put her hand on my head then and pulled it against her, and I guess I cried, though I ain't much to brag on that.

That shamed me, the crying did. When I got to my feet I was some taller than Mary, and I brushed those tears away, and felt worse about crying than anything else. So I took my blankets and went away to the edge of the circle and started to spread them out.

Something moved out there in the dark, and I took out my Shawk & McLanahan, for those two weeks had put me on edge. Whoever was out there went away.

The next morning when I was saddling up, Big Jack McGarry came by. He looked down at me and his eyes were mighty mean. "Figure you're a big man now, don't you? I'll slap some of that out of you!"

Right then I was some scared, but the pistol was in my belt and I knew if he started for me I'd pull iron. I didn't want to, but I would.

"You got my pap killed," I told him, "just like you figured on. If he was here you'd not talk about whuppin' me. I notice you never tried to come it over him."

He started his horse at me and raised his quirt, and just about that time a gun clicked behind me and I heard a voice say, "Go ahead, hit him. This wagon train can wait long enough to bury a man."

McGarry sat there with his quirt raised up and had the look of a fool.

It was that slim man in the buckskin shirt. He had a six-shooter in his hand and he was not fooling. "McGarry," he said, "if anything happens to that boy while I'm with this wagon train, even if it's an out-and-out accident, I'll kill you."

McGarry lowered his quirt and rode off to the head of the column. Only he was not there officially any more. They had voted him out of the captain's job.

The man in the buckskin shirt walked over to me and looked at me thoughtfully. "Boy," he said, "you're mighty young to be packin' a gun, but you'd better keep it handy."

14

"All right, sir."

"My name is Logan Pollard." He studied me a minute. "Tell me what happened back there. When your father was killed."

So for the first time I told the whole story.

He questioned me right sharp, then he knocked out his pipe and told me, quiet-like, "You'll do, boy. But don't use that gun unless you have to."

He went away then, and the next morning when the column moved out he came by on horseback. He motioned me to follow and I went with him and we rode out away from the wagons.

It wasn't until we were over the hill that he said, "We'll get an antelope or two, and we'll start your education same time."

"I can read. I been to school."

"Not that kind of education." He looked at me from that narrow brown face that never seemed to smile. "The kind you'll need. I'm going to teach you how to read sign, how to tell an Indian's tribe from his moccasins, and where to find game. Also, how to use that gun. I'm going to teach you things you need to know. So don't think of riding off by yourself just yet."

We rode on a ways farther, and then he drew up, indicating a plant about four feet high. It had a prickly look, with sort of white flowers shading off to violet.

"Indian thistle," he said, "and the roots will keep a man alive if there's nothing else to eat. Don't forget it."

He rode on, leading the way, pointing out things as we rode. Toward evening we circled back and we had two antelope.

"Back home," he said, "we had almost two thousand books. I read most of them. But this,"—he swept his arm wide to take in the country—"this is the book I like best. You can always learn. There's always something new on the page."

When he left me, he said, "Don't despise the Indian. He's lived here a long time, lived well. Learn from him."

15

THREE

The second day it was different. That morning he came for me right after the wagons started, but we rode fast, rode on ahead. As we rode, he told me things. They were things to remember, and Pollard did no aimless talking.

"Stalking a deer," he said, "you remember you can move as long as he has his head down, feeding. Just before he looks up he'll start to switch his tail. Stop moving then and stand right still, or sink down and wait until he starts to feed again.

"Indians often smoke their bodies in sage to kill body odor when going on a hunt. Mint will do the same thing, or any grass or plant that smells."

We were several miles ahead of the wagon train and far off to one side when we drew up in a grove of aspen. Ever seen aspen growing? Most times they grow in thick clumps, grow straight up, their trunks almost all of a size.

Logan Pollard swung down and I followed him. Then he paced about fifty feet from an aspen about four inches in diameter. "Take out your gun," he said, "and hold it down by your side."

He faced the slim young aspen and drew his own gun. "Now," he said, "lift your gun in line with that aspen trunk. Just keep lifting it at arm's length until your gun is shoulder high."

17

When I had done that a few times he had me take the shells from my gun. For over an hour we worked. He kept me at it, lifting that six-shooter and sighting along the barrel. Lifting it straight up from the base of the tree trunk until it was at eye level, always sighting along the barrel and keeping it in line with the trunk. Not until I'd been at it a few minutes longer did he start me snapping the gun when it reached shooting position.

"Every day," he said, "you'll practice that. Every day we'll ride out here."

"Will you teach me to draw real fast?" I asked him. That was something I wanted to know. I'd heard talk of Jack Slade and others who were mighty good that way.

"Not yet." He squatted on his heels. "First you learn how to use a gun. The draw isn't so important as it is to hit what you shoot at. Learn to make that first shot count. You may," he added dryly, "never get another."

He taught me to look where I was shooting and not at the gun, and to shoot as a man points a finger, and how to hang my holster so my palm came to the gun butt naturally. "No man," he said, "ever uses a gun unless he has to. Don't hunt trouble. Sooner or later you'll always find more than you want. A gun is a tool, mighty handy when you need it, and to be left alone until you do need it."

Beyond the shining mountains there was desert, and at its edge we left the wagon train.

"We'll be in California, Rye," Mary Tatum said. "If you want to come, you're welcome."

"Another time, ma'am. I'm riding south with Pollard."

She looked past me at Logan, who sat slim and straight on the black horse he rode. "Take care of him, Logan. He might have been my son."

"You're a child yourself, Mary. Too young to have had this boy. Maybe when he comes, I'll come with him."

She looked up at him and her cheeks were a little pinkish

under the tan. "Come, then, Logan Pollard. There's a welcome for you, too."

So we watched them start off toward the Salt Lake and the distant Pilot Butte, beyond the horizon. "If she couldn't marry Pap," I said, "I'd rather it would be you."

Pollard looked at me, but he did not smile. Only his eyes were friendly-like. "Rye," he said, "that was a nice thing you said."

South we rode then, and he showed me Brown's Hole, where the trappers used to rendezvous, and we rode through the rugged country and down to Santa Fe. Only it wasn't all riding, and it wasn't all easy. Every day he drilled me with the gun, and somehow I began to get the feel of it. My hands had always had a feel for a gun butt, and the big six-shooter began to handle easier. I could draw fast and shoot straight.

We lived off the country. Logan Pollard showed me how to rig snares and traps for small game, how to make a moose call, and what to use for bait when fishing. He showed me how to make a pot out of birch bark in which a man could boil water as long as the flame was kept below the water-level in the pot. He showed me how to build fires and he taught me to use wood ashes for baking powder in making biscuits.

Sometimes we would split up and travel alone all day, meeting only at night, and then I would have to rustle my own grub, and often as not track him to where we were to meet.

When he would ride on ahead and have me track him down, I would practice with the gun while waiting to start out. It had a natural, easy feel in my hand. I tried drawing and turning to fire as I drew. But Logan Pollard told me to respect a gun, too.

"They make them to kill," he said, "and you can kill yourself or somebody you love just as easy as an enemy. Every gun you haven't personally unloaded that minute should be treated as a loaded gun. Guns aren't supposed to be empty."

Santa Fe was a big town to me, the biggest since the wagon train left Missouri, and bigger than any town I'd seen up to then, except St. Louis.

There in Santa Fe I took a job herding a small bunch of cattle for a man, keeping them inside the boundary creek and out of the canyon. It was lazy, easy work most of the time. He paid me ten dollars a month, and after two months of it Logan Pollard came around to see me.

"You need some boots," he said, "and a new shirt."

He bought them for me from a pocketful of gold coins, and then went to a Mexican place he knew and ate a good Mexican meal, chicken with rice and black beans. Only he made me tuck my gun down inside my pants, and I wore it like that when I was in Santa Fe.

One day when I was with the cattle he rode out to see me and he took a book out of his saddlebags.

"Read it," he said. "Read it five times. You'll like it better each time. It's some stories about great men, and more great men have read this book than any other."

"Who wrote it?"

"Plutarch," he said, "and you can read it in the saddle."

It was warm and pleasant in the sunshine those days, and I read while I sat the saddle, or loafed under a tree sometimes, making an occasional circle to hold the stock in. And then one day two Mexicans rode up with a mean look in their eyes, and they fretted me some, looking over the cattle like they did.

One of them rode out and started to bunch the cattle, so I put Plutarch in the saddlebag and got up on Old Blue.

He walked out there mighty slow. I figure Old Blue knew more than me, and he could smell trouble making up before it hit.

We were halfway out there before they saw us, and they hesitated a moment, and then, getting a better look, they laughed.

"*Niño*," he said, and kept bunching the cows. And as I drew nearer they started them moving away from me, toward the creek.

"Leave those cows," I said. "Get away from here!"

They paid me no mind and I was getting scared. I'd been set

to watch those cows, and if anything happened to them it would be my fault. They were driving them toward the creek when I raced Old Blue ahead and turned them back.

The big Mexican with the scar on his face swore at me in Spanish and raced at me with a quirt. He raced up and I pulled Old Blue over and he swung, lashing at me. He struck me across the face, and I pulled the Shawk & McLanahan out of my pants.

His eyes got very big, and me, I was shaking all over, but that gun was as big in my fist as his.

He began to talk at me in Spanish and back off a little, and then the other Mexican rode over to see what was happening. When he saw the gun he stopped and looked very serious, and then he turned away from me as if to ride off, but when he turned he suddenly swung backhanded with his rope and the gun was torn from my hand and sent flying. Then he came at me, and he hit me across the face with the rope, and then lashed me with it over the back, and the half-coiled rope struck like a club and knocked me from my horse.

Then he spat on me and laughed and they drove off the cows, taking Old Blue along with them, and I lay there on the ground and could do nothing at all.

When I could get up I was very stiff and there was blood on me, but I walked to where the Shawk & McLanahan lay and picked it up.

It was ten miles back to town, but I walked it, and asked around for Pollard. When I found him he was playing cards. He waved at me and said, "Later, Rye. I'm busy now."

The place was crowded with men and some of them stared at my bloody face and the dirt on me, and I was ashamed. They would laugh at me if I told them I'd been knocked off my horse and had my cattle run off. So I went and borrowed a horse and took out after those Mexicans.

It was not only the cows; my mother's picture was in the saddlebags, and the Plutarch. And the Joslyn carbine was in the boot on Old Blue.

That night I didn't come up with them, or the next, but the third night I did.

They were around a water hole where there were some cottonwoods. It was the only water around and I was almighty thirsty, but I looked for Old Blue and saw him picketed off to one side.

It was dark and I was hungry, and they had a fire going and some grub, and I shucked the old Shawk & McLanahan out of my pants and cocked her.

The click of that gun cocking sounded loud in the night, and I said, not too loud, "You sit mighty still. I've come for my horse and cows."

"*El Niño,*" the scarred Mexican said.

I stepped into the light with the gun cocked.

"Kill him," the scarred Mexican said. "Kill him and they will think he took the cattle himself. Kill him and bury him here."

The other Mexican was sneaking a hand toward a gun

"Stop!" I said it loud, and I guess my voice sounded shrill.

He just dived at the gun, and I shot, and the bullet knocked him rolling. He sprawled out and the other Mexican lunged at me, and I tried to burn him, but before I could shoot there was a shot from the edge of the brush, and then another.

The Mexican diving at me fell face down, all sprawled out, and then he rolled over and there was a blue hole between his eyes, and the first Mexican, the one I shot, had another bullet that had torn off the side of his face after it killed him.

Logan Pollard stood there with a gun in his hand, his face as still and cold as always.

"You should have told me, Rye. I didn't realize you'd had trouble until one of the men said you were bloody. Then I started after you."

We walked over and looked down at the Mexican I had shot. My bullet was a little high . . . but not much.

Pollard looked at me strangely, then caught up Old Blue and we started the cows toward home.

The next day he told me to quit, and when I collected my

money I had thirty-two dollars, all told. With that in my pocket, and the money from my Pap, which I'd never touched yet, I felt rich. We started northwest into the wild country around the San Juan, following the old Spanish Trail.

"We're going to California to see Mary Tatum," he said, "and then maybe you can go to school. You're too willing to use a gun."

"They stole the cows," I said.

"I know."

"And Ma's picture."

He glanced at me. "Oh, I see."

It was a wild and lonely land of great red walls and massive buttes. There were canyons knifed deep in the rocky crust of the earth, and cactus with red flowers, and there were Indians, but they seemed friendly enough, and we traveled on, me riding Old Blue.

The sun rose hot and high in the mornings, and sometimes we took all morning to get to the bottom of a canyon, then all afternoon climbing out. We crossed wide red deserts and camped in lonely places by tiny water holes, and my face grew browner and leaner and I learned more of the country. And one morning I got up and looked over at Logan Pollard.

"Today I'm fourteen," I said.

"Fourteen. Too young to live like this," he said. "A man needs the refining influences of feminine companionship."

He was a careful man. Careful of his walk, careful of the way he dressed, careful when he handled guns, and careful in the care of his horse. Every morning he brushed the dust from his clothes, and every morning he combed his hair.

And when we rode he talked to me about Shakespeare and the Bible, and some about Plutarch and Plato. Some of it I didn't set much store by, but most of it made a kind of sense.

From Virginia, he'd come. Educated there, and then he'd come west.

"Why?"

"There was a man killed. They thought I did it."

"Did you?"

"Yes. I shot him fair, in a duel."

We rode on for several miles. I liked watching the shadows of the clouds on the desert. "I was to have married his sister. He didn't want me to."

And in California I went to school.

Logan Pollard stayed around for a while, and then he rode away. I did not believe Mary Tatum wanted him to go.

Yet he was gone no more than a week before he came back, and when I came riding in on Old Blue I saw them talking, serious-like, on the porch. "It has happened before," he was saying, "and it may happen again."

"Not here," she told him. "This is a quiet place."

"All right," he said finally. "I'll stay."

The winter passed and all summer long I worked, felling logs for a lumber mill and holding down a riding job on a nearby ranch the rest of the time. In the fall and winter I went to school and learned how to work problems and something of history. Most of all, I liked to read Plutarch.

Logan Pollard rode out to see me one day. I was sitting on a log, reading my nooning away.

"Third time," I said. "I read slow."

"This is a book to be read that way. Taste it, roll the flavor on your tongue."

It was not only school and reading. I was growing, too, and some part of every day I went out into the woods and practiced with the gun. I'd a natural gift for guns, and my skill had increased rapidly. Pollard never mentioned guns to me now, and was no longer wearing his. Not in sight, anyway.

These were good months. Work never worried me. I enjoyed using my muscles, liked feeling strong, and there was always a little time for riding in the mountains, tracking stray cattle or horses, hunting varmints that preyed on the stock.

It was spring again and Old Blue kept looking at me, and I knew he expected me to saddle up and ride. It was spring, and

24

I was fifteen years old, close to six feet tall, but thin. Only my shoulders and arms were strong, and my hands.

"What happened to the gun?" Logan asked me.

So I reached down in my pants and brought it out, that old Shawk & McLanahan .36 Pap had given me.

"Ever shoot it?"

"Yes," I said, and turning the muzzle, I fired. It was all one easy move. Sixty yards away a pine cone shattered into bits. Pollard looked at me and nodded. "You can shoot. I only hope you never have to."

He was married that next Sunday to Mary Tatum, and I stood up with them, feeling awkward in a store-bought broadcloth suit and a stiff collar, the first I ever owned. And when it was over and we ate the cake, Mary said, "We want you to stay with us, Rye. If you can't be my son, be my brother."

So I stayed on.

When two months more had passed I mounted Old Blue and rode down to the store. It was mighty pretty that morning, and the sun was bright, and every leaf was like a tiny mirror. The water of the stream rippled and rollicked over the stones, and it seemed the world had never been so nice.

I was wearing my broadcloth suit because I was going to a pie supper before I came home.

At the store I bought some crackers and cheese and went to the steps to eat, and there I was sitting real quiet when a big man rode up on a white horse. He was thick in the middle and his vest was dirty with food stains, and when he saw Old Blue he fetched up short and stopped.

He got down from the saddle and he walked slow around that horse. He glanced over at me, only my head was down and he couldn't make out my face, and I was eating.

"Who owns this horse?"

He said it real loud, his voice mighty big and important-like. There were two men settin' up on the porch and they said nothing, so he looked over at me. "Who owns this horse?"

Stuffing the last of the cheese and crackers in my mouth, I

got up. "I own him, McGarry. You want to make something out of that?"

His nose was blue-veined and bigger than I'd remembered, and his eyes were even smaller and more piggish. He was a wide man, the sleeves of his dirty white shirt rolled halfway to his elbows, his big boots scuffed and worn. His hat was too small for his big head and he was unshaved and dirty.

"You? You, is it?"

"It's me," I said, and suddenly I knew I hated this man. I was wondering, too, if he realized Mary Tatum was in town. Or that she was married to Logan Pollard.

"It was you made all that trouble," he said. "I ain't had no luck since. You an' that little skirt your pap played with."

Right then I hit him. I hit him on the mouth and he staggered back two steps and almost fell. Blood started to come and he grabbed for his gun.

Then something bucked in my hand and he stepped back and sat down as my gun bucked again, and he was settin' there dead almost half a minute before he rolled over on his face and stretched out, but in that last split second of life I saw shocked surprise on his face. And there I stood with that old Shawk & McLanahan in my hand and Big Jack McGarry dead at my feet.

FOUR

Mary Tatum was feeding the chickens when I rode into the yard. She looked up and I saw her eyes widen a little, and she came up to me as I got down.

"Rye, what is it? What's happened?"

So I stood there, feeling a sinking in me, hating to tell her, yet knowing I had to.

"Mary," I said, "I killed a man."

"Oh, *no!*" She caught my arm. "Not you, Rye!"

"Yes, ma'am. I killed Jack McGarry."

That stopped her, and she held my arm a minute, her gray eyes searching mine. "Jack McGarry? *Here?*"

"Yes, ma'am. He said words. . . . He reached for his gun after I hit him."

"Words, Rye?"

"Yes, ma'am. He spoke slighting of you and Pap."

"Oh. We had better tell Logan."

Somehow Logan did not seem surprised. He listened to me and I told it plain and simple, holding nothing back. "I reckon," I said honestly, "it was partly because I hated him."

There was something else on his mind. "He touched his gun first?"

"Yes, sir. He had it almost out when I shot him."

Nothing more was said and Mary went about getting supper.

27

She was never one to take on when it was past time for it to do any good. We ate some, although I didn't have much appetite, and kept seeing how McGarry looked, lying there on the ground with that shocked expression on his face. I didn't hate him any more, I didn't feel anything about him except maybe sad that he had pushed me into it. I didn't want to shoot anybody any more.

We went out on the porch and Logan began to talk. First off, it seemed like he was just telling us about his boyhood and his travels, and then it came to me that this was something special, for me. It was a lesson, like.

He had killed a man at nineteen. The man was a riverboat gambler. Then he killed his sweetheart's brother, because back there, them days, if a man called you out, you went, or you left the country wearing the coward brand.

Afterward he left the country, anyway. He had killed four men in gun battles, he said, and he told me he hoped never to kill another, and then he said, "Rye, you're a hand with a gun. Maybe the best I ever saw. You've a natural skill, a natural eye, and you judge distance easy and fine. That's a responsibility, Rye. This is a time when all men carry guns. Naturally, some are better than others, just like some men can use an ax better, or make a better wheel, like your pap. But a gun is different, because with a gun you can kill."

He paused a minute, looking down at his fine brown hands, the sort of hands you might expect to see on a violinist. "You'll have to use a gun, from time to time. So be careful that you use it right. Never draw a gun unless you mean to shoot, never shoot unless you shoot to kill.

"Back there with the Mexicans you were too slow to shoot. If I hadn't been there you might have been killed. Yet I'd rather have you shoot too slow than have you too ready to shoot. Never kill the wrong man or it will punish you all the days of your life."

He was right about that, and I knew it. I was no fool kid who

28

thought a gun made me a big man. Right then I didn't ever figure to kill anybody else, anytime.

Morning came, and when I walked out to saddle up there was a big, rawboned roan coming into the yard with a man on his back. The man had a shock of uncut hair and a big mustache. His hat was small and he looked sort of funny, but there was a badge on his chest that was not funny, and he wore a pistol.

Logan came to the door, and Mary. She looked white and scared, but Logan was like he always was, quiet and sort of stern.

The man on the roan wore a checked shirt and it was untidy. He wore suspenders, too.

"Name of Balcher," he said, and he took some chewing tobacco from his shirt pocket. "Carry it there," he said, sort of smiling, "so nobody will mistake I'm reaching for a gun. I'd sure hate," he added, "to be shot by mistake."

"What's your business, Mr. Balcher?" Logan stepped down off the porch.

Balcher looked at him thoughtfully. "My!" he said. "For a quiet man I sure run into a lot of you folks. You're one of them, too, sure's shootin'."

Logan stood quiet, waiting. Balcher turned his big head and looked at me, chewing slow. "How old are you, boy?"

"Fifteen. Going on sixteen."

He rolled his squid in his jaw. "Young," he said, "but you handle a gun like a growed man. You killed that feller yestiddy."

"Yes, sir."

He studied me carefully. "You know him before?"

Logan Pollard interrupted, and quietly he told the story of what happened on the trail, leaving out nothing. He made it plain that I had reason to feel as I did, and that McGarry had opened the trouble, not I.

Balcher listened, looking from Logan to me with lonesome hound-dog eyes.

"Reckon I'd feel like shootin' him myself." He turned in his

29

saddle. "Don't blame you, son. Understand that. Don't blame you a bit. But you got to go."

"Go?" Mary said. "But he can't, Sheriff! He's like my own brother! This is his home!"

The way she said it made a lump come in my throat and I was afraid it was bringing tears to my eyes. I reckon there was nobody quite so nice as Mary.

" 'Fraid so." Balcher said it regretfully. "I ain't much hand with a gun, myself. Reckon either one of you could shoot me dead before I could touch iron, but the way I keep the peace about here is to send all gun folks apackin'.

"Now don't get me wrong. I got nothin' against you, Tyler, but folks know you're handy with a gun now. Some rambunctious youngster is liable to want to find out if he's better. So I reckon you better ride."

The sun was bright on the hard-packed earth of the ranchyard. It was warm and pleasant, standing there, a trickle of water falling in the trough, the smell of coffee from the house. This was home for me. The only home I'd had for a long, long time. And now they were telling me to go.

"And if he doesn't?" Logan asked the question, his voice low and hard.

Balcher shrugged. "Well, I can't shoot him. Folks down to town say they never saw anything as fast as this Rye Tyler. He shucked his gun so fast nobody scarce seen it. An' he didn't miss once he got it out. I reckon if the bullet hadn't killed McGarry, the shock would have, he was that surprised."

Balcher turned in his saddle. "Look, Mr. Pollard. I got to keep the peace. She's my job. I reckon I'm too lazy to farm, and nothing much grows for me, anyway. But, four years now I kep' the peace. I hope, folks, that he'll ride out quiet. If he don't, I got to go back down to town and round up eight or ten of the folks with shotguns to start him movin'. To do that I'd have to spoil a day's work for a lot of folks. Now, you wouldn't want that, would you?"

"I reckon not, Mr. Balcher," I said. "I reckon I can go."

"Rye!" Mary protested.

"Got to, Mary. You know I got to. It's all right. I been sort of itchin' to see more country, and Old Blue, he's been downright disappointed in me."

Daybreak I taken the road out to Surprise Valley, across the mountains and north. I figured I might hunt a little, then maybe get a riding job before I headed south. Right then I had twenty-six dollars of my own money, and I was still carrying the forty dollars Pap left me.

Saying good-bye to Mary was worst of all. She clung to my sleeve and she kissed me, and I reckon it was the first time since I was a mite of a baby I'd been kissed. It was kind of sweet-like, and the feel of it stayed on my cheek all the way across the mountain.

Logan rode a ways with me, then he shook hands and said, "Come see us, Rye. This is home, always."

Two miles down the trail I saw a man on a roan horse setting out there in plain sight. He was setting sideways on that horse when I came up to him, and he grinned at me, sort of sly. It was Balcher. He put his hands on the pommel and said, "Boy, I wish you luck. You take it easy with that gun. You're a fine boy, so don't you start to shootin' less you have to."

Then I rode down the trail, and a lump was in my throat and in my heart, too, and my stomach was all empty. This was the second time I'd lost folks that loved me. First Pap, by Indian guns, and now Mary and Logan, by my own gun.

Was that the way it was going to be?

Do you know that Western land? Do you know the far plains and the high, snow-crested ridges? Do you know the beaver streams, the water laughing in the bright sun? Do you know the sound of wind in the pines? The cloud shadows on the desert's face? Have you stood on a high ridge and looked fifty miles across the country, country known only to Indians, antelope, and buffalo?

Have you crawled out of your bedroll in the chill of a spring morning with the crisp air fresh in your lungs and the sound of running water in your ears? Have you started a fire and made coffee, and broiled your venison over an open fire? Have you smelled ironwood burning, or cedar?

That was how I lived for a whole year after I left Mary and Logan. I lived away from men, riding, drifting, and reading Plutarch for the fourth time.

Washington, Oregon, Idaho, Montana, Wyoming, and down to Colorado.

Beside campfires under the icy Teton peaks, I read of Hannibal and of Cato. I smelled the smoke of a hundred campfires, as I drifted.

Rarely did I find a white man's fire, and only occasionally one left by an Indian. I saw the country of the Nez Percés and the Blackfeet, of the Crows, the Shoshones, and the Sioux. I wandered up the lost red canyons of the La Sal Mountains, and through the Abajo Range.

The only sounds I heard were the sounds that the wilderness makes. The slap of warning from a beaver's tail on water, the sudden crash and rush of an elk, the harsh, throaty snarl of a mountain lion . . . the wind, the water, and the storm.

The shelters I had were caves or corners among the trees, or wickiups I built myself. All that Logan Pollard had taught me came in handy, and I learned more.

And so after many days I came again to a town where there were people. I rode to the edge of the hill and looked down, a little frightened, a little uncertain. And I knew that I had changed. Some of the stillness of the mountains was in me, some of the pace of the far forests, but there was also the old thing that lived in me always. But I could be alone no longer. It was time to return to the world of people, and so I started Old Blue down the slope.

FIVE

My shirt was buckskin. My breeches were buckskin. My boots had long since worn to nothing and been replaced by moccasins. I still carried the old Joslyn carbine, and I still carried the Shawk & McLanahan .36. So I rode into town to sell my furs.

Right then I was nigh seventeen. I was an inch over six feet and I weighed one hundred and seventy pounds, and no bit of fat on my bones. Lean and tough as any old catamount, wearing a torn and battered hat, I must have been a sight to see. Into that town I came, riding slow.

Old Blue was beginning to feel the miles. He was getting some years on him, too. But he loved the life as I did and he could still run neck and neck with a buffalo while I shot.

The town was a booming mine camp, the street lined with a jostling crowd of booted, belted men. Leaving Old Blue at the livery-stable hitch rail, I walked up the street, happy to be among people again, even if I knew none of them. Yet I walked aloof, for I hesitated to meet people or to make friends. There was always in the back of my mind the thought of the gun, and I did not wish to fire in anger at any man.

Oddly enough, in those long wilderness months I had no trouble with Indians. I had wandered their country, shared their hunting grounds, but evaded contact with them. A few times I had gone into the Nez Percé villages to trade for things I needed.

It was warm and sunny in the street. Leaning against an awning post, I watched the people pass. Tents and false-fronted stores, a long log bunkhouse that called itself a hotel, and a bigger log building that was a saloon. Down the street a man sold whisky from a board laid across two barrels, dipping the whisky with a tin cup.

And it was good to be there. These were tough and bearded men, a rough, roistering, and on the whole friendly crowd. They were men, and I was a man among them. My face was lean and hard, and my body was lean, too. Only my shoulders were wide, my chest deep, my arms strong. Those long months in the mountains had put some beef on me, and tempered my strength.

A man came up the street wearing a badge. He had a broad brown face with strong cheek and jawbones, the skin of his face stretched tight. His eyes were deep-sunk and gray to almost white.

He looked hard at me, then looked again. It was a long, slow look that measured and assayed me, but he continued to walk. Farther down the street he stopped and I saw him standing alone, watching me.

Finally he moved on, but when he did a slim young man walked over and stopped beside me. "Don't know you, friend, but watch yourself. Ollie Burdette's got his eye on you."

"Trouble?"

"He's the marshal, and he shoots first and asks questions later. Killed a man last week."

"Thanks."

"My name's Kipp. Got a little spread out east of town. Come out, if you've a mind to."

He walked on away from me, a quiet young man with quick intelligent eyes. But maybe too quick to warn me.

For a while I loafed where I was, thinking about it. Right now I should ride on, but I'd just come into town and had done nothing, nor did I intend to get on the wrong side of the law, ever. Sometimes the law can make mistakes, but usually it's right, and it's needed to regulate those who haven't yet learned how to live with their fellow men.

Walking across the street, I went into the hotel. The dining room was only half full, so I found a table and sat down.

After I'd ordered, I picked up an old newspaper and browsed through it. I was just getting to the last page when a voice said, "Please? May I have it?"

Looking up from the paper, I saw a slender young girl. She could have been no more than fourteen, but she had beautiful eyes and a nice smile.

I got to my feet quickly, embarrassed. "Yes, ma'am. Of course. I just finished."

"It was Papa's paper. I put it down on the table and forgot. He would be just furious if I didn't have it. He loves his newspaper."

"Sorry, ma'am. I didn't know."

Suddenly someone was beside us. Glancing around, I looked into those gray-white eyes of Ollie Burdette's. They were cold and still. "This man botherin' you, young lady?"

His voice was harsh, commanding. There was something almost brutal in its tone and assurance. It was the voice of a man not only ready for trouble, but pushing it.

"Oh, no!" She smiled quickly. "Of course he isn't! He just gave me my newspaper. I'd have lost it otherwise."

"All right." He turned away almost reluctantly, giving me a hard look, and I felt the hairs prickle on the back of my neck, and my mouth was dry. Yet it angered me, too. Burdette was very ready to find trouble.

"Are you looking for a job?"

My eyes went back to her. She was looking up at me, bright and eager. "Papa needs a man to break horses."

"I'd like that. Where's your place?"

She told me, then added, "I'm Liza Hetrick. You ask for me."

35

When she was gone and my dinner finished I sat there thinking. What Kipp had said might be true. There were gunmen who deliberately hunted trouble, some because of an urge to kill, some because they wanted to stop trouble before it began, some who were building a reputation or whose only claim to recognition was a list of killings. But why pick on me? Because I was only a boy and wore a man's gun?

Yet I was no longer a boy in Western consideration. At seventeen and younger, a boy wore a man's boots and a man's responsibilities. And was the better for it, I thought.

Yet it would be a good idea to ride out of town. Avoiding trouble was the best thing. I wasn't trying to prove anything to anybody. I wasn't so insecure that I had to make people realize I was a tough man, and no man in his right mind hunts trouble.

Walking to the door after paying my check, I looked down the street. Burdette was a block away, standing in front of the barbershop. Stepping out of the door, I walked down the street to my horse. As I gathered the reins I heard his boots on the walk.

"You, there!" His voice was harsh. "Don't I know you?"

When I turned around it was very slowly. I could feel a queer stillness in me, something I'd never felt before. His cold eyes stared into mine.

"Don't believe you do, Mr. Burdette. I'm new here."

"I've seen you somewhere. I know that look."

I sat my horse and looked at him. "You've never seen me, Mr. Burdette. I'm only a boy and I've lived most of my life in the hills. But I think the look is one you've seen before."

With that I touched my spurs and started away. But he was not through. "Wait!"

Drawing up, I looked at him. All along the street movement had stopped. We were the center of attention. That strange, cool, remote feeling was in me. That waiting. . . .

"What d'you mean by that?" He came into the street, but not close. "And where did you get my name?"

"Your name was told me," I said, "and also that you killed a man last week." Why I said it I'll never know, but it wasn't in me to be bullied, and Burdette was making me angry. "Don't ride me, Burdette. If you want to kill a man this week, try somebody else!"

And then I rode out of town.

The trail wound upward into the tall pines. The grass smelled good, and there were flowers along the way. At the fifth turning, just four miles from town, I saw a rail fence and back of it a barn bigger than any I'd ever seen, and a strongly built log house.

A dog ran out, barking. Then a tall, rough-hewn man with a shock of white hair came to the door. "Light and set, stranger! I'm Frank Hetrick."

"My name is Ryan Tyler. I was told to ask for Liza."

He turned. "Liza! Here's your beau!"

She came to the door, poised and pretty, her cheeks pink under the tan. "Papa! You shouldn't say such things. I told him you'd give him a job."

Hetrick looked at me from keen blue eyes. "Do you break horses, Tyler?"

"Yes, sir. If you want them broke gentle."

"Of course." The remark pleased him. "Get down and come in."

At the door I took off my ragged black hat and ran my fingers through my hair. There were carpets on the floor and the furniture was finished off and varnished. You didn't see much of that in pioneer country.

It was the first time I'd been inside a house in over a year, and I'd never been in one as nice as this before. Not, at least, since Pap and I left home. There was a double row of books on shelves across the room, and when Hetrick left the room I walked over to look.

Some of them were books Logan Pollard had talked about. Tacitus, Thucydides, Plato, and a dozen others that were mostly history.

37

Hetrick returned to the room and noticed my interest. "I see you like books. Do you read a lot?"

"No, sir. But I had a friend who talked about books to me."

After supper we went out on the porch to sit and Hetrick built a smudge to fight off the mosquitoes. We sat there talking for a while and watching the black shadows capture the mountains. But that smudge was almost as bad as the mosquitoes, so we went in.

Liza sat down beside me and started asking questions, and the first thing I knew I had told them about Logan Pollard and Mary, and how Pap died. But I didn't tell them about the Indians I killed, or about the Mexican rustlers, or about McGarry.

It wasn't that I wanted to hide anything, but I wasn't the kind to talk, and that was over and done. The one thing I did not want was a gun-fighting reputation, and besides, I liked these people. Somehow, I felt at home here. I liked Hetrick, and Liza was a mighty nice girl, even if she did look so big-eyed at me sometimes that I was embarrassed.

The next day I went to work at forty a month. There was one other hand on the place, a Mexican named Miguel.

Hetrick came out and watched us that first day. And from time to time in the days that followed he came around and watched, but he had no comment and made no suggestions. Only one day he stopped me. "Rye," he said, "I like your work."

"Thanks, sir."

"You're working well and you're working fast."

"You've good stock," I said, and meant it. "Breeding in these horses. It shows."

"Yes." He looked at me thoughtfully. "Breeding always shows through." He changed the subject suddenly. "Rye, Liza told me you had words with Ollie Burdette."

"It was nothing."

"Be careful. He's a killer, Rye. He's dangerous. You've known horses like that, and I've watched Burdette. He's got a drive in him, a drive to kill."

"Yes, sir."

Twice during the following month, Kipp came over. He liked to talk and he liked Mrs. Hetrick's pies. So did I. He was over for my birthday, too, the day I was eighteen.

He looked at my old Shawk & McLanahan. "You should have a Colt," he said. "They're a mighty fine gun."

"Heard of them," I admitted. "I'd like one."

The next morning when we went out, nine of Hetrick's best horses were gone. Stolen.

The story was all there, in the tracks around the corral where we held the freshly broken stock. Moving around, careful to spoil no tracks, I worked it out. "There's two, at least," I said. "Probably one or two more."

Kipp had stayed the night, and when I went to the barn for my saddle, he followed along. "I'll go with you," he said. "Three is better than two."

Reading their sign was no problem. I'd been living too long like an Indian. The three of us rode fast, knowing as we did that they were going clear out of the country. We could tell that from the direction they took. There was nothing that way, nothing at all for miles.

Hetrick had a fine new rifle, and Kipp was well armed. As for me, I still had the old Joslyn .50, although it was pretty nigh worn out now. But I knew that old carbine and could make it talk.

The thieves took the horses into a stream and followed it for miles, but that isn't the trick some folks think it is, and it didn't wipe out their trail the way they expected. A horse makes a deep track in wet sand and sometimes the tracks don't wash out very soon.

So water or not, we held to their trail until they left the stream and took out across a sandy flat. From that they reached some prairie, but the dew was wet on the grass and the horses had knocked the grass down and you could follow it at a trot.

On the fourth day of trailing the thieves had slowed down. We were coming up fast until we smelled a wood fire, and then we started walking our horses. We were going down a long slope covered with pines when we saw the branding fire.

We bunched a little as we neared the fire and they were busy and didn't see us until a horse whinnied. One man dropped his branding iron and a thin trail of smoke lifted from the grass where the iron fell.

There were four of them, four to our three. They stood waiting for us as we walked our horses nearer, four tough looking men from the rough country. One of them was a lean, hatchet-faced man with hair that curled over his shirt collar. He had gray-striped trousers tucked into his boot tops.

"Reckon you got the wrong horses," I said.

The big man with the black beard looked nervously at the one with the hatchet face. I was watching him, too. He had a bronco look about him that spelled trouble, and I could see it plain. He wore his gun tied down and his right hand was ready. And they were four to our three.

"You think so?" Hatchet Face was doing the talking.

One of the others was an Indian or a breed, a square-jawed man with a wide face and a beaded vest.

"The horses belong to Hetrick, here. I broke them all. We're taking them back."

"Are you, now?" Hatchet Face smiled and showed some teeth missing. "You're a long ways from home, boys, and we've got the number on you. That means we keep the horses."

Kipp and Hetrick were forgotten. I could feel that lonely feeling again, the feeling of trouble coming, and of being poised and ready for it. It was the something that happened to me when something was coming up.

"No," I said, choosing my words careful-like. "You are four to three, but with us it's just one to one."

Hetrick had a wife and daughter, and I knew he was no fighting man, although he would be right with me when the chips were down. I wanted to keep this short and quick, and I had an idea that I might do it by keeping the fight between the two of us. The others didn't look ambitious about a shoot-out.

Black Beard would back up quick if he had the chance. The man I'd called was number one and if there was to be a fight, he would make it.

His face thinned down, seemed to sharpen. He had not expected that. There was a quick calculation in his eyes.

Old Blue walked forward two steps, then stopped. I was looking right down the muzzle of his courage.

"Yes." I said it low and straight at him. "You have this wrong, Bronco. I'm the man you think you are."

He measured me, not liking it. "What's that mean?"

"It means we take our horses. It means if you reach for a gun, I'll kill you."

Never before had I talked like that to any man. Nor did I know where the confidence came from, but it was there, as it had been when Logan Pollard stopped McGarry that day when he would have quirted me.

Bronco was bothered, but he was still confident. So I gave him time. I wanted his sand to run out. Maybe it would. And there was an even better chance it would not, for whoever Bronco was, he had used his gun; I could sense it, feel it.

That feeling sharpened all my senses, set me up and ready for what would come. Yet there was no hanging back. The horses were ours, and no man would dare walk away from such a situation and still call himself a man. Not in the West, not in our day. And we weren't about to walk away. Hetrick and Kipp would have got themselves killed, but this time they had the difference, and I was the difference.

"Mr. Hetrick," I said, "you and Kipp gather up the horses."

"Like hell!" Bronco flared.

Shorty nervously shifted his feet, and that did it. Maybe Bronco thought Shorty was starting something. Anyway, his hand swept back and I shot him.

The bullet cut the Bull Durham tag hanging from his shirt pocket. The second bullet struck an inch lower and right.

His gun was half drawn, but he seemed to shove it down in his holster and he started to take a step, and then he was dead.

41

A crow cawed out in the trees on the slope. A horse stamped. The other men stood flat-footed, caught that way, unmoving, not wanting to move.

And there was no more fight. Even if they had wanted one, it was too late. My gun was out and they were under it, and few men have the stomach to buck that deal.

"I'll get the horses," Kipp said, and he started for them.

Hetrick got down from his saddle. "Rye," he said, "we'd better collect their guns."

"Sure," I said.

Shorty stared at me. "Rye," he said thoughtfully. "I never heard that name. Know who you killed?"

"A horse thief," I said.

"You killed Rice Wheeler," he said, "the Panhandle gunman."

"He should have stayed in the Panhandle," I said.

SIX

Returning was only a two-day trip. We had no trail to find, and we could cut across country, which we did. Nobody had very much to say that first day out.

Late on the second day, when we were walking our horses up a long canyon, Kipp said, "That Wheeler, he killed six or seven men." Nobody said anything to that, and he went on. "Wait until I tell this in town! It'll make Ollie Burdette turn green."

"Don't tell him!" Hetrick said angrily. "Don't say a word about it. I got back my horses and let's let it lay."

"But why not? It isn't every day a man kills a Rice Wheeler!"

"You don't know gunmen," Hetrick said testily. "It will start Burdette hunting the boy all the more."

Reluctantly Kipp agreed, but only after I said, "I don't want that kind of talk about me, I'm not making any reputation."

All the way home I was thinking it out. I had killed another man. This was two. That Mexican . . . My shot might have killed him, but it was Pollard's shot that did kill him. No doubt about that. And I didn't want to claim any more than I had to.

Liza ran out to meet us as we came up. "You got the horses!" She was excited. "Did you catch the thieves? Where are they?"

Later, I guess she was told, or she heard about it, because for several days she was very big-eyed around me. But she didn't say anything to me about it, or to anyone else. And it wasn't even mentioned for a long time.

Sometimes at night we would sit over the table and talk, and I'd tell them stories about living in the mountains alone, and of some of the places I'd seen. And once when we were talking I went to my saddlebags and got out Ma's picture and showed it to them.

She was a pretty woman. Only twenty when the picture was taken.

Mrs. Hetrick looked at it for a long time, then at me. "Do you know anything about her family?"

"No, ma'am. Pap told me that when they were married her family sort of got shut of her. I mean . . . well, the way I heard it, they didn't think Pap had money enough. But Pap and Ma, they were happy."

Mrs. Hetrick put the picture down thoughtfully. "That dress she had on . . . that was expensive."

I knew nothing about women's clothes. It looked just like any dress to me. Women, I guess they know about things like that. One time, a few days later, I heard her telling Hetrick, "Real lace. I never saw a prettier collar. It's a pity the boy doesn't know her family."

Sometimes of an evening Liza and I would walk down to the spring and talk, or out by the corral. Always in plain sight of the house. She was a mighty pretty youngster, but just a youngster. Me, I was eighteen, headin' on for nineteen.

We'd talk long talks there by that corral, leaning on the bars close to Old Blue. We'd talk boy-girl talk, even though she was younger than me. About what we wanted to do, the dreams we had, and where we wanted to go. We both wanted to be rich, but I guess that wasn't very important to us, either. It was just that we both wanted more things, and to see more.

Liza would listen, all wide-eyed and excited when I talked about the mountains up in Wyoming. Or the Blues over in Oregon, or those wild, empty canyons that cut down through the southwest corner of Utah.

44

Twice I went to town, but only once did I see Burdette. The other time he was out of town chasing down some outlaw. He brought back his horse with an empty saddle.

The time I did see him I was coming out of the store with some supplies to load into the buckboard. He came down to the walk to watch me load up.

"Breaking horses for Hetrick, I hear."

"That's right. Nice stock."

"Hear you lost some."

"Found 'em again."

"Any trouble?"

His eyes were searching mine. It gave me the feeling he might have heard something, but either wasn't sure or didn't believe what he had heard.

"Nothing to speak of."

"Lucky. I heard Rice Wheeler was working these hills."

By that time I was up on the seat, turning the team. Liza was there beside me and she looked up at Burdette. "He isn't any more," she said, and before he could question that, I got the team started out of town.

"You shouldn't have said that," I told her. "Now he won't rest until he digs out the story."

"I don't care," she said pertly. "I don't like him."

It was nice driving along over the trail, talking to Liza. We always had something to say to each other and it was hard to realize she was growing up, too.

And my time to leave was not far off. Hetrick had much to do yet to make his place pay. He would have a fine bunch of horses to sell, and he had some good breeding stock. So he had a good chance of building something really worth while. It made me see what a man could do. When all the rest of them were hunting gold or silver, running saloons or gambling houses, he was quietly building a ranch and a horse herd. It was something stable, something that could last.

But once the horses were broken he would need me no longer, and it was time I started to find a place for myself in the world. And a ranch was what I wanted, too. My own ranch, somewhere back in some of those green valleys I'd seen during my wandering.

When I had broken the last horse, a sorrel with three stockings, I went to Hetrick.

"Finished," I said.

He opened a drawer in his desk and took out some money. He paid me what he owed me. Not counting what I had drawn on my wages, I had seventy dollars coming to me. And I'd still not touched the forty dollars Pap left me. I still had that, sewed into my gun belt.

"Wish I could keep you on, son. There just isn't work enough."

"I know."

"Come around whenever you like, Rye. We enjoy having you." He pushed his desk drawer shut. "Got any plans?"

"Yes, sir. I thought . . . well, I heard tell of some placer diggings down on Willow. I figured to try that. Maybe . . . well, I don't aim to ride aimless all my life long. I had an idea that if I could get a stake I'd start ranching."

"That's wise." Hetrick hesitated, then he said, "Son, be careful around town. Kipp got drunk the other night and Burdette got the story out of him. He knows you killed Rice Wheeler."

"I'm sorry."

"So am I. But Liza told us she had said something to him about it."

"It was nothing. I don't blame her."

"It started him asking questions. You'll have to be careful." He took out his pipe and filled it. "Rye, you watch him. He's killed three men at the Crossing. He's . . . well, he's tricky."

"All right, sir. But I don't expect to be around there."

The next morning after breakfast I rode away. Liza did not come out to say good-bye, but I could hear her in the next room. It sounded as if she was crying. I sort of felt like crying myself. Only men don't carry on.

46

When I was turning into the lane she ran out and waved. I was going to miss her.

It was thirty miles to Willow Creek, and it was far away from anywhere. Once there, I scouted along the creek and picked a likely-looking bench. It was my first time to try hunting gold, but I'd heard talk of it, and around Pollard's place in California they had taken thousands from the creeks.

The work was lonely and hard. The bench was on a curve of the Willow, and I found a little color. I sank a shaft to bedrock, which was only eight feet down, and I cleaned up the bedrock and panned it out. After two weeks of brutal labor I had taken out about ninety dollars.

Not much, but better than punching cows. It was harder living alone now than it had been in the mountains before I met the Hetricks. They were good people, and I'd liked staying there with them, and I thought a lot about Liza. It was Liza I kept remembering. The way she laughed, how she smiled, and the warm way her eyes looked sometimes.

The next week I cleaned out some seams in the bedrock and took out more than two hundred dollars in twenty minutes.

It was spotty. There was a lot of black sand mixed in with the gold and it was hard to get the gold out. Twice in the following week I moved upstream, working bars and benches to the tune of a little color here and a little more there.

My grub ran short, but I killed an elk and jerked the meat, then caught a few fish from time to time. Living off the country was almost second nature to me by this time.

Nobody came around. Once a couple of Utes came by and I gave them some of my coffee. When they left, one of them told me about a bench upstream that I should try.

Taking a chance that they knew what they were talking about, I went upstream the next morning and found the bench. It was hidden in the pines that flanked both sides of the stream, and it was above the water.

There was an old caved-in shaft there, a shovel with the handle long gone, and a miserable little dugout in the bank. I found some arrowheads around. Whoever had mined here must have been here twenty years ago. This was Indian country then.

When I cleaned out the old shaft I panned some of the bottom gravel and washed out twelve dollars in a few minutes. The second pan was off bedrock and ran to twenty-six dollars. Working like all get-out, I cleaned up a good bit of dust. Not enough to make a man rich, but more money than I ever had before.

When I finished that week I loaded my gear and saddled up. Old Blue was fat and sassy, so we drifted back to the Crossing.

The old black hat was still on my head, and I was wearing buckskins. It wasn't trouble I was looking for, but I remembered Hetrick's warning. Outside of town I reined in and got out the old Shawk & McLanahan and belted it on.

When I swung down at the bank, Burdette was coming down the street, and when they had finished weighing out my gold they counted out my money and it came to just $462. And I still had $50 of my wages from Hetrick.

"Doing well," Burdette said.

"Not bad."

"So you killed Rice Wheeler?"

"Uh-huh."

"That was what you meant, then? When you said I should know the look of you?"

I shrugged. "Read it any way you like."

He watched me as I walked out to my horse and stepped into the leather. When I rode toward Hetrick's, he was still watching. I could feel his eyes on me and I'll admit I didn't like it. At a store on the edge of town I bought some ribbon for Liza, and I'd also saved her a small gold nugget.

She ran out to the gate to see me, recognizing Old Blue from far down the road. She stepped up in my stirrup and rode that way up to the house. Mrs. Hetrick was at the door, drying her hands on her apron, and Hetrick came up from the corral, smiling a greeting. I felt all choked up. I guess it was the first time anybody felt good about seeing me come back. Most of my life I've been a stranger.

It was good to walk around the place again and to see the horses. One of them, a tall Appaloosa, followed me along the fence, whinnying at me, much to Old Blue's disgust.

While we waited for dinner and talked about the horses, Hetrick suddenly asked, "Did you see Burdette?"

"I saw him."

"Bother you?"

"No."

"He wanted to buy a horse from me, but I turned him down. I've seen the way he treats his horses."

That gave me some satisfaction, but it worried me, too. I wouldn't want any of the horses I had broken so carefully to get into the hands of Ollie Burdette, who was, as Hetrick said, a hard man with a horse. But it worried me because I knew that Hetrick, a stiff-necked man and stern about such things, would not have hesitated to tell Burdette what he thought.

It was pleasant inside the house, and Mrs. Hetrick put on a linen tablecloth and had the table fixed up real fancy. When I had my hair slicked down as much as it would ever slick, which isn't much, I sat down to the best supper I'd had.

Kipp rode in while I was there, all excited about the gold I'd panned out, but I knew he wouldn't be so much excited by the work. It was a good supper and there was good talk around, and had I been their own son, I couldn't have been treated any better.

"That Burdette," Kipp said suddenly, "I don't think he's in your class. He's fast, all right, but not as fast as you."

Hetrick frowned. He never liked talk about gun fighters, but Kipp was always talking of Clay Allison, the Cimarron gun fighter, or the Earps, Bill Longley, Langford Peel, or John Bull.

"You'd match any of them," he said, his excitement showing. "I'd like to see you up against Hardin, or this Bonney feller, down in New Mexico."

"Why, Kipp." Mrs. Hetrick was horrified. "A body would think you'd like to see a man killed!"

He looked startled, and his face flushed. "It ain't that," he said hurriedly. "It's just . . . well, sort of like . . . I don't know," he finished lamely. "I just like to see who's best."

Talk like that worried me some, and I didn't want any more of it. Loose-talking folks have promoted more than one fight that would never have happened otherwise.

Kipp wasn't the only one. When I was around town I'd heard some talk, folks speculating on who would win, Burdette or me. The talk excited them. It wasn't that they were blood-thirsty, just that they liked a contest, and they just didn't think that a man would have to die to decide it.

Or maybe they did. Maybe they figured the sooner we killed each other off, the better.

It nagged at a man's mind. Was he better than me? I didn't want to be better than anybody, not at all. But it worried me some because I wanted to live.

Even nice people warned me, never realizing that even their warnings were an incitement. It was on their minds, on all their minds, so how could it be different with me? Or with Burdette? The sooner I got out of town, the better.

"I'm taking out," I said suddenly. "I figure to go East. Have a ride on the cars, maybe. I want to see St. Louis or Kansas City. Maybe New Orleans."

"Will you look up your family?" Mrs. Hetrick asked.

"I reckon not. They never tried to find me."

"You don't know," she protested. "Maybe they think you're dead. Maybe they don't even know about you."

"Just as well. They didn't set much store by Ma, or they'd not have thrown her over like that."

"Maybe they were sorry, Rye. People make mistakes. You have some money now, why don't you look them up?"

No matter about that, I was getting out of here. I didn't want to hear any more talk about Ollie Burdette, or whether he was faster than me.

So we talked it out, and I made up my mind to leave Old Blue behind. He was all of eleven years old, maybe even older. It was time he had a rest. I'd ride one of Hetrick's horses over the mountains to the railroad and sell him there. We agreed on that.

Hetrick wanted Old Blue. He was gentle enough and would be a good horse for Liza to ride, and she liked him. I said I'd rather see her have him than anybody else, and she flushed a little and looked all bright-eyed. She was a nice little girl. And I was going to miss her. I was going to miss her a lot.

Come daylight, I saddled up.

Burdette was standing on the street when I rode into the Crossing with Hetrick. He saw the bedroll behind my saddle.

"Leavin'?"

"Going East," I said. "I want to see some country."

"Better stay shut of Dodge. They eat little boys down there."

It rankled, and suddenly I felt something hot and ugly rise inside me. I turned on him. "You hungry?" I said.

It surprised him and he didn't like it. We were close up, and he didn't like that. We weren't four feet apart, and neither of us could miss. Right then I stepped closer. It was a fool thing to do, but right at the moment, I was doing it. I crowded him. "You hungry?" I repeated. "You want to eat this little boy?"

He backed up, his face gray. He wasn't scared. I knew he wasn't scared. It was just that nobody could win if the shooting started. It was too close. It was belly to belly. He wasn't scared, he just wanted to win. He didn't want to get shot, and he was older than me, old enough to be cautious. Later I would have better judgment, but right then I was mad.

"Any time," I said. "Just any time."

Those gray eyes were ugly. He hated me so bad it hurt, and he wanted to draw. He wanted to kill me. But he laughed, and he made it sound easy, though it must have been hard to do.

"You got me wrong, kid. I was just foolin'."

But he was not fooling. It just wasn't the right time, and Ollie Burdette figured he could wait.

"Sure," I said. "Forget it."

So I left him like that and I rode out of town and down the trail.

Maybe I would look up my relatives, after all.

When I looked back, Ollie Burdette still stood there, but Hetrick was gone.

Right then I had a hunch. "I'll see you again, Ollie Burdette, I'll bet on it."

And there was an unspoken thought that it would be the last time . . . for one of us.

SEVEN

Market Square in Kansas City was hustling and booming when I first walked down the street. To me it was a big town, all crowded with people, all seeming in a big hurry.

I liked seeing the beer wagons with their big Percheron or Clydesdale teams, and I liked watching the fancy carriages with their fine driving horses all neck-reined up and prancing along. And right away I noticed that nobody carried a gun where you could see it, so I stashed mine away behind my waistband.

For hours I just walked the streets, looking at all the things I didn't want. I never saw so much I could do without, and never so many people. Right away I saw I'd have to do something about my buckskins. Even the new black hat I'd bought looked shabby, so I went to a tailor and had him make me up a fine gray suit and one of black, and I bought a fine white hat, some shirts with ruffled fronts, and some black string ties. When I'd found some boots of black calfskin I began to feel mighty dressed up.

Almost nineteen, I could pass as several years older. I was weighing one hundred and eighty now, and no ounce of fat on me. Once in a while I'd pass some girl who would look at me, then turn to look again. And I always saw it because I'd usually turned to look myself.

The old Shawk & McLanahan was still with me, but seeing

some of the Bisley Colts, I longed for a new and more efficient gun. Several times I almost went in to buy one, but each time I hesitated. Right now I needed no gun and there was a lot I wanted to see on the money I had left.

One day on Market Square I saw a bunch of men sitting or standing around a bench. Some of them looked Western, so I walked over, and when I got there they were talking about shooting. It was warm, and most of them had their coats off. One tall, finely built man with long hair to his shoulders and a mustache interested me. He was wide across the cheekbones and had gray eyes.

Several times I saw him studying me, and whenever I was around, I noticed he knew where I was.

There was a young fellow standing near me and he whispered out of the corner of his mouth, "Wild Bill's trying to figure out who you are."

"Wild Bill? Is that Hickok?"

"Sure thing. He's a fine shot."

This fellow stood there listening to the talk of guns and shooting, and then he turned to me. "Have you eaten yet? I'm hungry."

We walked along together. He was a buffalo hunter, he told me, and he had come into Kansas City with nearly three thousand dollars from his hides. "My name's Dixon," he said. "Billy Dixon."

"I'm Ryan Tyler . . . lately from Colorado."

We ate together, then went to see a show. Later we met a strong-built man, older than us, whom Dixon had known on the prairie. His name was Kirk Jordan.

Several days we hung around town, but my money was running short and I'd begun to think about leaving. When I was sitting on the Square one day, a sharp-faced man in a black coat stopped near me. Several times he looked me over carefully. Me, I'd hunted a good bit myself, and knew how a hunter looked. This man was hunting something.

He sat down near me, and after a bit he opened a conversation. After a while he mentioned poker . . . a friendly game.

Now, I'm not so smart as some, but Logan Pollard had taught me a sight of poker. And he taught me how to win at poker, and how a cardsharp works. Pollard was good. He knew a lot, and being naturally clever with my hands, I had learned fast.

Moreover, poker isn't a very friendly game. If you play poker, you play for money, and beyond a certain point there is nothing friendly about money. So when a stranger suggests a friendly game of poker . . . well, you figure it out.

This fellow had me pegged right. He figured I was in from the hills, had bought some fancy clothes, and was carrying a stake in my pocket. Only the last was a wrong guess.

"Don't really play cards," I said cautiously, "but if you're going to play, I'd enjoy watching."

"Come along, then."

We started off, and glancing back, I saw Hickok and Jim Hanrahan and some others looking after us with amused smiles. They were thinking that I would learn a lesson, and every man has some lessons to learn for himself.

There were five men in the game and one of them looked like a buffalo hunter. The others . . . well, I didn't know about them. But after a while, I sat in.

They let me win three out of four times. Each time the win was small, but it was enough to double what I had to begin with.

I played a blundering, careless game, sizing up the others. The way I saw it, all but two were cardsharps. The buffalo hunter was named Billy Ogg, and there was a man who had been a stage driver in Texas. A mighty fine fellow.

On the fifth hand they built the pot pretty strong and I stayed with them, and lost.

It was my deal then, and clumsily I gathered in the cards, having a hard time getting them arranged, but in the process I got two aces on the bottom. Shuffling the cards, I managed to get another ace to the bottom, and then I dealt the cards, taking my three aces off the bottom as I needed them. That is, I dealt myself two of them to begin; then when I drew three cards, one of them was the third ace.

Woods, the man who had roped me into the game, raised five dollars. I saw him and raised again. Woods raised and I went along, and at the showdown my three aces took the pot.

Woods didn't say anything, but he looked angry, and one of the others, a fat, dirty man, growled something under his breath. It was a good pot, more than seventy dollars, as I recall.

We played for two hours, and I was careful. When a hand looked too good to be true, I wouldn't go along or played it so badly that I lost little, and when I dealt or could hold out a card or two, I won. At the end of that time I was four hundred dollars ahead, and Woods was getting mighty ugly.

Right about that time I decided enough was enough. There had to be a break, and I wanted to make it when I was ready, not have Woods or one of the others make it and catch me off balance. Pushing back my chair, I said, "Got to get some sleep. I'm quitting."

"You can't quit now!" Woods protested. "You've got our money."

My smile didn't make him any happier. Nor did what I said. "And that wasn't the way you planned it, was it?"

Woods's face went red and the fat man's hand dropped to his lap. Only I'd seen the gun under the napkin almost an hour before. My old Shawk & McLanahan was out and covering them and I sort of stepped back a little.

"You," I said to Ogg. "You've been taken. So's he." I indicated the stage driver. "You two pick up the pot."

"Like hell!" Woods started to get up.

My gun muzzle swung to him. "I'd as soon kill you," I said pleasantly. "Don't make it necessary."

Ogg and the stage driver scooped up the money. Both of them had been in twice as deep as I could have gone, and most of the money was theirs. They gathered it up and went to the door, but at the door Billy Ogg shucked his own gun. "Come on, Tyler. I'd as soon kill one of them my own self."

The three of us walked out together. The stage driver was Johnny Keeler, and they split a thousand between them and insisted I take the two hundred that remained. I refused.

Ogg glanced skeptically at the old Shawk & McLanahan. "Does that thing shoot? I didn't think they made them any more."

"It shoots."

"I'm beginning to get this now," Keeler said suddenly. "You're Rye Tyler, the Colorado gun fighter."

"I'm from Colorado," I said.

"You killed Rice Wheeler?"

"He stole horses from my boss."

Billy Ogg looked me over thoughtfully. "Now, that's mighty interestin'. T'other day down to Tom Speers' place, Hickok said you were a gun fighter. Said he could read it in you."

"You'll have to come around and meet the boys," Keeler said. "Wyatt Earp's in town, too."

"I'm going to New Orleans," I said.

Next morning early I woke up, bathed, shaved, and got slicked up. Just as I was starting to pack there was a knock on the door. When I opened it there was a man standing there with a box in his hands, and a rifle.

The rifle was a new .44 Henry repeater, the finest made. And in the box were two of the hard-to-get Smith & Wesson Russians, the pistol that was breaking all the target records.

Behind the man came Billy Ogg and Johnny Keeler. "A present from us," Ogg said, grinning at my surprise. "You saved our money. This is a present."

Long after I was on the river boat, headed downriver for New Orleans, I handled those guns. Yet it was with something like regret that I packed away the old Shawk & McLanahan. It had been with me a long time.

For two weeks I loafed in New Orleans, seeing the sights,

eating the best meals, sometimes playing cards a little. But this was honest playing, for I played with honest men, and I lost a little, won a little, and at the end of two weeks had won back half what I'd spent around town.

New Orleans was a lively place, and I liked it, but I was getting restless to leave. The West was my country, and I had to be doing something. Nowhere in the world was there anything that belonged to me, nor did I have any place to call home. Also, I kept thinking about Liza. She would be sixteen now, and girls married at sixteen. The thought of her marrying somebody made me feel kind of panicky and scared, as if I was losing something I needed.

Finally I packed to go, and then while I was waiting for time to leave, I went to a gambling hall called the Wolf Trap. As soon as I was inside the door I saw Woods, and with him a local tough known as Chris Lillie. Wanting no trouble, I turned at once and went out.

The streets were dark and silent. It was very late and few people were about. Walking swiftly, I was almost to the end of the street when I heard someone running behind me. Quickly I ducked into a doorway.

Nobody passed, and nobody came near. Yet I had heard those feet. Suddenly I remembered that at this point another street, a very narrow one, intersected the one on which I had been walking. It would be on that other street that I'd heard the running.

Deliberately I crossed the street away from the corner. Cities were new to me, but the hunting of men is much the same anywhere. In the blackness of a doorway I waited, watching the point where the two streets came together.

Several minutes passed and then I saw Chris Lillie come out of the alley and peer down the street up which I had come. The street was, of course, empty.

All was dark and still except under the few misty street lights. Fog was beginning to drift in from the bottoms, and the night was ghostly in its silence.

Then a second man emerged, and this was Woods. They stood there together, whispering and peering around. My disappearance worried them. And then I stepped out into the street. "Looking for me?" I asked.

Woods had a pistol in his hand. He whipped it up and fired, but he shot too quickly, and missed. I felt the bullet whip past me as I steadied my aim and fired. Woods turned back, starting in the direction from which he had come, and then fell dead.

Lillie sprinted for the alley, and I let him go. Waiting only a minute longer, I turned away and walked back to my hotel. By daybreak I was riding a rented horse west of the river. And I had killed my third white man.

But this time with the Smith & Wesson .44, not the old Shawk & McLanahan.

EIGHT

In 1872 much of Texas was still wild. In eastern Texas there were vast thickets of chaparral, and some good forests. It was lonely country, dangerous for a stranger. It was feuding country, too. The Lee-Peacock and Sutton-Taylor feuds had left the country split wide open. Neither of them was really settled, and much of the bloodiest fighting was still to come.

Every ranch in some sections of eastern Texas was an armed camp, and few men rode alone. There were old enmities that had survived the fights of the Regulators and the Moderators, and the fighting and general lawlessness had brought into the country some bad men from the Indian Territory and elsewhere. But Texas had enough of her own.

In Marshall I bought a horse. He was a fine dappled gray, the fastest walking horse I ever saw. He was seventeen hands high and could really step out and move, ideal for such a trip as this.

Some nights I camped out, and at times stayed in wayside inns or at ranches. It was good riding, and new country for me. In the back of my mind all the while was the thought that I was heading for Colorado, where I'd stay a while before riding on to California to visit Logan and Mary. Meanwhile I was young and restless, and the country looked good.

For a month I rode, drifting south and a little west, and one day I came on a man with a herd of cows.

61

He had six hundred head and he was short-handed. He was a big man with a blunt, good-natured face. He looked me over as I came along the road, then called out, "Hunting a job?"

"Use one," I said, and swung my gray alongside him.

"Thirty a month," he said. "I'm driving to Uvalde. Selling this herd to Bill Bennett. He's going up the trail to Kansas."

"All right."

"Can't promise you Kansas, but the job is good to Uvalde. My name is Wilson."

The gray was quick, intelligent, and active. He became a good cow horse, and learned fast. Mostly, though, I rode one of Wilson's horses.

Nobody asked questions in those days. Every man was judged by what he did. Lots of men had pasts they did not want examined, and if you minded your own business and did your work, nobody bothered about anything else.

Riding jobs always suited me. I liked to think, and a man could follow along with a herd of cattle and do a powerful lot of thinking. In my jeans I had over a thousand dollars. Here and there along the trail I'd gambled some, and I'd won and lost, but I had a stake. And I wanted more.

The beef Wilson had was mostly young stuff, and it looked good. In Kansas City I'd heard a lot of talk about the rich grass of the northern prairies and how cattle could actually fatten while on the trail. This stuff Wilson was driving was young, rawboned, and would fill out.

The third day I made up my mind. Wilson was riding point and I drifted alongside the herd until I pulled abreast of him. After we'd passed the time of day and talked about the weather and how dusty it was, I started in. "Got a little money," I said. "Mind if I buy a few cows and drift them with yours? I'd be a partner in the herd then, and you'd have a free cow hand."

"Go ahead!" Wilson waved a hand. "Glad to have you!"

Leaving the herd that night, I rode on ahead and began to check the ranches. And right away I began to wish I had more money.

Cash was a scarce thing in Texas in those days. Men had cattle, horses, and hay, but real cash money was mighty hard to come by for the average rancher. Moreover, he had to gamble on riding anywhere from thirty to a hundred miles to market with maybe no sale when he got there, or a niggardly price.

I rode into a ranch yard and drifted my horse up to the trough. Looking around at the cattle, I saw they were mostly good stock, with a few culls here and there such as you'll find in any cow outfit. But this stock was big, like your longhorns are apt to be, and rangy. Given a chance, a longhorn could fill out to quite a lot of beef.

Grass was not good and most of the range was overstocked. Most of the ranchers had not begun to realize that there was a limit to the amount of stock the range could carry. Their great argument was a buffalo. They had themselves seen the range black with their millions. I had seen it, too, but what I remembered that some of them seemed to forget was that the buffalo never stopped moving. They gave the grass a chance to grow back. It was a different thing with cattle. They were confined to one range, once men began to herd them, and they ate the grass to nothing.

My horse walked up to the trough and started to drink, and a long-geared man in boots with run-down heels walked over from the corral.

"Light an' set," he invited me. "Don't get many visitors hereabouts."

"Riding through," I told him as I swung down. "I'm going to Uvalde."

"What I ought to do," he said, biting off a chew, "I should drift me a herd up to San Antone. But that takes hands, and I ain't got 'em. I'd like to drift a herd to Kansas."

"Risky," I said. "Indians, herd cutters, an' such-like."

His wife came out to look at me, and two wide-eyed children in homemade dresses.

"Might buy a few myself," I said thoughtfully. "I'm ridin' through. Shame to make the trip for nothin'."

He glanced at me. My rig was new and looked good and prosperous. "You could do worse," he said. "Fact is, if a man had him a little cash money he could buy cows mighty cheap."

"Don't know," I said doubtfully. "A man could lose a sight of money thataway. Stampedes . . . Men have made money goin' over the trail, but they've lost it, too. Lost their shirts, some of 'em."

"Young fellow like you," the rancher said, "he should take a chance if anybody should. Got your life ahead of you. I reckon you could double your money."

"Well," I hesitated, "I have got a little money, but gold is scarce in this country and I hate to get shut of it." I let that settle down through his thinking for a few minutes, and then added, "Why, a man can buy most anything for gold in this country!"

"Gold?" He looked at me again. "Mister, if you want to buy cows with gold, you don't have to go any farther. They pay ten dollars a head in San Antone. Now I—"

"More'n I'd pay. A man's got risks, driving to Kansas. He has to hire riders, get a chuck wagon, grub, a string of horses. Takes a sight of money."

The rancher chewed slowly, looking thoughtful. "Might sell a few," he said. "Could use some cash money."

Cattle bred like rabbits and his range was overstocked. He would have been a fool not to sell, if only to save grass for the other cows.

"Give you five dollars a head?"

He was astonished. "*Five?* You're crazy."

I gathered my reins and moved to mount. "Maybe I'd better forget it, anyway. As it is, I'm drawing cow hand's pay. If I own cows, I stand to lose. I'll just forget it."

"Might let a few go for eight dollars?" he suggested hopefully.

"No," I said, "I've got to ride on. Enjoyed the talk."

He put a hand on my saddle. "Now, look—"

A half hour later we compromised at seven dollars a head, his men to round them up, and no culls. I bought a hundred head. And when Wilson came along, I swung them into the herd. A neighbor boy who wanted to see San Antonio came along for the ten dollars I promised him to make the drive.

It was a good feeling, seeing those cattle, knowing they were mine. They were good stock, and would bring a good price whether I sold them in San Antonio or at the end of the trail in Kansas.

William J. Bennett was waiting in the plaza at Uvalde when I rode my horse into the square with Wilson. Wilson gestured to me. "Ryan Tyler," he said, "a good hand."

"Glad to know you." Bennett cut the end from his cigar. "Got any cows?"

"A hundred head."

"I'll buy 'em."

As easy as that I could turn a profit, maybe double my money, and in only a few days of work. I might go out again and buy more cattle and sell them, too. If I worked hard and used my head, I could build a business for myself. But the trail to Kansas was north, and it was closer to Colorado.

"Ten dollars a head," Bennett said. "Take it or leave it."

"No," I said, taking my time. "I don't want to sell. I want to make the drive with you." I leaned on the pommel. "Mr. Bennett, I want an outfit of my own. I know a little valley out in Colorado that's just what I want, but I need money. If I can sell those cattle in Kansas, I'll be well along toward having my stake."

He rolled his cigar in his teeth and looked around the plaza. Finally he took the cigar from his mouth. "Have you any more money?"

"Just a few hundred dollars."

"You want to buy more cattle?"

"Yes, sir."

He looked at the end of his cigar. "All right, Tyler." He reached in his pocket and took out a small sack. "There's a

65

thousand dollars in that. Buy cattle for me, too. We want to leave here by the fifth."

As I started to swing my horse, he spoke again, only just loud enough for me to hear. "You the man who killed Rice Wheeler?"

For a moment I sat very still in the saddle. Then looking around at him, I nodded.

"Knew him," Bennett spoke abruptly. "He killed my saddle partner at Red River Crossing four years ago."

Riding out of town, I felt the weight of that sack of gold. It was the first time anyone had ever trusted me with money, and he had merely turned and tossed it to me. Yet it was more than trust of money. He was trusting my judgment to buy well. It gave me a good feeling.

A week later I had bought few cattle. The areas close to San Antonio had been swept clean, and all I had been able to send in were thirty head, all good stock but nothing like what we wanted for the drive. So I pushed on, hoping for better luck.

The country was wild and lonely, occasional chaparral, but mostly open country, broken and rugged. Ranches were scattered, and some of the small ones were merely rawhide outfits without enough cows to bother with. The air changed and it began to look like rain.

By nightfall the clouds were hanging low and they were spitting a little rain, so I started the gray to moving along and dug my slicker out of my bedroll. I'd taken to wearing both guns, but only one in its holster. The other I tucked behind my waistband, the butt out of sight under the edge of my coat. It was added insurance, because I was carrying another man's money and was never one for trusting to luck. I'd helped bury a few men who did.

This was rough country in more ways than one. During any day's ride a man would come up to several horsemen, mighty hard-looking men. Most of them, by the look of them, had been up the creek and over the mountain.

The wind was blowing, splattering rain ahead of it, and I was thinking of something to crawl into when I heard cattle. Just the restlessness of a good-sized bunch, and some lowing from cows. Then I saw the hard outline of a roof gable, and just off the road loomed a large house. In a flash of lightning it showed itself square and solid, built of sawed lumber.

To one side there were corrals and a lean-to, and beyond, in an open place that was walled on three sides by bluffs, was the herd. Catching glimpses by the heat lightning, I saw the steers were big and rangy, and they looked like young stock. It was a herd that might run to six hundred head.

And then the rain hit. She swept in with a roar, the solid sheets of water striking like blows on a shoulder, and I raced the gray to the lean-to and swung down. Here, partly out of the storm, it was quieter except for the roar of rain drumming on the roof. The lean-to was partly faced, and there was shelter for several horses. I found a place and tied the gray, and then I slopped, head down against the rain, to the house.

There was a light gleaming faintly behind a shutter, so I banged on the door.

Nothing happened.

I was standing in the rain, as there was no porch, only a slab of rock for a doorstep. Dropping my hand to the latch, I pressed it and stepped in, closing the door. I was about to call out when I heard voices. I heard a man saying, "You pay us now or we take the herd."

"You've no right!" It was a woman's voice, protesting. "You were to be paid when the herd was delivered and sold."

Outside rain drummed on the roof. I hesitated, feeling guilty and uncertain of what to do, but the conversation held my attention. It was also my business. This was cow talk and I was looking for cows.

"We done changed our minds."

In the tone of the man's voice there was something hard, faintly sneering. It was a voice I did not like, and quite obviously the voice of a man talking to a woman with no man standing by.

"Then I'll simply get someone else to handle the herd. After they're sold, you'll be paid."

"We ain't gonna wait." The man's voice was confident, amused. "Anyway, who would you get? Ain't nobody gonna handle them cows if we say they ain't."

I felt mighty like a fool, standing there. But this woman had a herd to sell, and it looked mighty like I'd be doing her a favor to buy it right now. But it was not going to make me any friends among those men.

"Anybody to home?" I called it out loud and there was silence afterward, so I walked through the door into the lighted room.

There were two women there. One—I guessed it was the one who had been doing the talking—was standing. She was young, and, in a plain sort of way, an attractive woman. The other woman was older. She looked frightened and worried.

There were three men, a rough-looking outfit, unshaved and dirty. All of them were looking at me.

"You didn't hear me knock," I said, taking off my hat with my left hand, "so I took the liberty of coming in out of the rain."

"Of course. . . . Won't you sit down?" The young woman's worry wasn't making her forget her hospitality. "We haven't much, but—"

"He won't be stayin'," the big man said abruptly. "We got business to talk. Nothin' for strangers to hear."

Before she could speak up, I took the issue by the quickest handle. "Heard some talk of selling cattle," I said. "I'm buying. How many and how much?"

The big man had heavy shoulders and a blunt, powerful jaw. There was a cross-eyed man and one in a gray shirt. They didn't like it. They didn't like me.

"You heard wrong." The big man did the talking. "We're selling in San Antone."

Ignoring him, I looked at the young woman. Her eyes were wary, but hopeful. "I take it you're the owner. I'll buy the cattle here and save you the drive. I'm buying for Bennett, and he's the only one buying in San Antone now."

From an easy steal it was beginning to look to the three men like a total loss. The big man was getting red around the gills and the others were showing their anger. So I took the play right away from them.

"Ma'am, coming in like I did, I couldn't help overhearing some of the talk. Seems you hired these men to round up the cattle, to pay them when the cows were sold. That right?"

"It is."

"Now you look here!" The big man stepped toward me, his lips thinned down.

"I'll buy your cattle," I said to the young woman. "I'll buy them as they stand according to your tally. I'll pay cash."

"I'll sell."

I swung one foot just enough to face all three of them. "The cattle are sold to me," I said. "You're fired."

"You—"

"Shut up!" I took an easy step toward the big man. "I'm paying you off right now. You worked for wages, and I'm paying your wages. Want to make something out of that?"

It had them flat-footed. I was no defenseless woman, and while I might look young, that gun on my hip was as old as his.

"We got no argument with you. You didn't hire us, you can't fire us."

My eyes stayed right where they were, on him. But I spoke to her. "Ma'am, will you sell me those cows?"

"You just bought them," she said quietly.

"The price," I said, "will be mutually agreeable."

The man in the gray shirt was inching his hand down. Some signal seemed to pass between them and the big man started to move. So I shucked my gun and laid the barrel across the side of his jaw. He went down as if he'd been hit with an ax, and my gun muzzle dropped on the other two.

"The fewer there are," I said, "the fewer I have to pay."

They wanted to try me. They wanted it so bad they could

taste it. Maybe if they both tried, they might take me, but somebody had to make a move—and nobody was anxious to die. And there is something about a man who knows what he intends to do, who knows what he can do. Burdette had seen it in me, and Logan Pollard had seen it long ago. These men could see it now, and they hesitated.

The man on the floor groaned. Slowly the gray-shirted man let his hand relax.

"Pick him up," I said, "and get out."

The man in the gray shirt hesitated. "What about our money?" he asked.

"They were to get thirty a month," the young woman said. "They worked about three weeks."

With my free hand I counted out twenty-five dollars per man. "Pick it up, and if one of you feels lucky, start something."

They could see I was young, but this was John Wesley Hardin's country, and he had killed twenty men by the time he was my age. They didn't like it, but I was too ready, so they picked up their money and got out.

I followed them to the door and watched them get their horses.

"Don't get any ideas about those cattle," I said. "If anything happens to them, or to any part of them, I'll hunt down all three of you and kill you where I find you."

Waiting in the doorway, I listened to them move down the road, then went back inside.

The two women were putting food on the table. The young woman turned on me. "Thanks," she said. "Thanks very much."

It embarrassed me, the way they were looking at me, so I said, "Seven dollars a head?"

"All right." She pushed the tally sheet across the table. It was for 637 head. "How will you get them to San Antone?"

"Hire riders."

"There's nobody. Those were the Tetlow boys. Nobody wants trouble with them."

"Rona, we might get Johnny," the older woman suggested, "and we can both ride."

"All right, Mom." Rona turned to me. "I've been riding since I was six. We can both help."

So it was like that, and I took the herd into San Antone with two women and a boy of fourteen helping me. But I had an old mossy-horn steer leading and he liked to travel. He was worth a half-dozen riders.

Bennett paid Rona himself, glancing at me from time to time. When he had paid her off, the two of them turned to go.

Rona held out her hand to me. "Thanks," she said. "They were all we had."

One of Bennett's hands came in. "Tyler," he said, "you want those cows—"

Something stopped him. I guess it was the way everybody looked. Everybody but me, that is. Bennett's face went kind of white, and both the women turned back again to look at me. We stood there like that, and I was wondering what was wrong.

And then Rona said, "Your name is Tyler?"

"Yes, ma'am," I said.

"Not *Ryan* Tyler?"

"Yes, ma'am."

She looked at me again, and then she said quietly, "Thanks. Thanks, Mr. Tyler." And then both women walked out.

Bennett took his cigar from his teeth and swore softly, bitterly. Then he put the cigar back in his mouth and he looked at me. "You know who they were?"

"Who?"

"That was Rice Wheeler's widow . . . and his mother."

NINE

We pointed them north across the dry prairie grass, three thousand head of them, big longhorns led by my tough old brindle steer. We pointed them north and took the trail, and it was a good feeling to be heading north and to know that I owned part of the drive; that at last I had a stake in something.

After the first week the cattle settled down to the pattern of the drive. Every morning at daybreak that old mossy-horn was on his feet and ready, and the first time a cow hand started out from the chuck wagon he turned his head north and started the herd.

It was a hard, tough life, and it took hard men to live it. From daylight to dark in the saddle, eating dust, fighting ornery cow stock, driving through occasional rainstorms and fording rivers that ran bank-full with tumbling water. But we kept them going.

Not too fast, for the grass was rich and we wanted them to take on weight. Sometimes for days at a time they just grazed north, moving the way buffalo moved, taking a mouthful of grass here, another there, but moving.

Two hundred and fifty head of that stock were mine, wearing no special brand. Depending on prices, I could hit the other end of the trail with between five and seven thousand dollars, and that was a lot of money. And it was real money, not gambling money.

New grass was turning the prairies gray-green, and there were bluebonnets massed for miles along the way the cattle walked, with here and there streaks of yellow mustard. The grazing was good, and the stock was taking on weight. If we got through without too much trouble, we would both make money.

Nothing was ever said about Rice Wheeler. Sometimes I wondered what they thought when they heard my name called and knew who I was. Bennett ventured the only comment, about two days out.

I'd cut out to head off a young steer who was getting ornery and trying to break from the herd. Bennett helped me turn him back, then turned in alongside me.

"Don't think about Wheeler," he said abruptly. "He was no good. Best thing ever happened to Rona, when he took off and never come back."

"Leave of his own accord?"

"No. Folks caught him with some fresh-worked brands in his herd. He killed a man and left ahead of the posse."

It was a good crew we had. The oldest of the lot, not speaking of the boss or the cook, was twenty-six. Two of the hands had just turned sixteen. And we had fourteen cow hands in all, seventeen with Bennett, the cook, and me.

We crossed the Red at Red River Station and pushed on into the Indian Territory, heading for Wichita.

Twice groups of Indians came down and each time we gave them a beef. Each time they wanted more, but they settled without argument.

After crossing the North Canadian we lost a hand in a stampede. We buried him there, high on a hill where he could listen to the coyotes and hear the night singing of the herders. He was seventeen the day he was killed.

The Osage drums were beating, and we held the herd close. We weren't looking for trouble, but we knew it could come. Nighttime we slept away from the fire, and we kept two men on watch near camp. We missed a lot of sleep, them days. But we were getting on toward the Kansas line, and things looked good.

When the first cows were coming up to the Cimarron we were attacked by a party of Osages. They came sweeping down on us from a wide-mouthed draw, a bunch of young bucks with more nerve than sense. And they hit us at the wrong time.

Me, the boss, and a tough hand called Mustang Roberts were riding drag. As though by command, we swung around, dropped to the ground, knelt, and took steady aim. Then we waited.

They came on fast, very fast, riding low down on their horses' sides. On signal, we fired.

An Indian fell, his horse catching him in the head with a hoof as he went over him. A horse went down, throwing his rider wide where a bullet from Kid Beaton's Sharps nailed him.

They lost three men and two horses in a matter of seconds, and drew off, deciding they'd had it.

Two days later Mustang went out after antelope and didn't come in. I was in the saddle, so I swung around and picked up his trail. When I'd followed him maybe five miles I heard the boom of a rifle.

It was far off in a bottom somewhere. Taking it fast, I headed toward the sound with that fine new Winchester of mine ready for action.

There were six of them, all Kiowas, and they had Mustang pinned down in a buffalo wallow with his horse dead and a bullet through his leg.

There was no chance for surprise. They would have heard my horse's hoofs drumming on the sod, and they would be ready for me. So I went in fast, the reins looped on the pommel and shooting as I came. I wasn't hitting anything, but I was dusting them some, and they didn't like it.

Maybe I did burn one of them, because he jumped and yelled. Then I went down into that buffalo wallow, riding fast, Mustang covering me. He nailed one of them just as I swung down to the wallow, and then he came up and I slid an arm around his waist as he put a boot in my stirrup.

Surprising thing was, we got away with it. We got clean out of there, with Mustang shooting back at them. Five of us came back later and picked up his saddle. We scouted some, and found a lot of blood on the grass at one point, a little at a couple of others.

"Killed one," Kid Beaton said. "Killed one sure."

And then there were days of dust and driving, and the grass thinning out a little. So we swung wide, taking a longer route, ducking the main trail, finding richer grass to keep the stock up. Twice we stopped and let them loaf and graze two days at a time. Bennett knew cattle, and he knew the markets.

We moved on. Crossing the Kansas line we found a long, shallow valley with good grass and a creek. We moved the herd into the valley and made camp near the creek, upstream from the herd in a bunch of willows and some cottonwoods, big old trees.

We were just finishing chuck when we heard the beat of horses' hoofs and four men rode up.

Mustang put his plate down and glanced over at me. "Watch yourself," he said.

Three of them got down. The leader was a small man with a thin face and quick, shifty eyes. The two backing him were tough, dirty men, one of them a breed.

"My name's Leet Bowers," the leader said. "Come daylight we're cutting your herd."

" 'Fraid you might have picked up some of our cattle . . . by mistake," another man said, grinning.

Bennett was quiet. He was standing there with his feet apart, holding his coffee cup. "Nobody cuts my herd," he said flatly.

Bowers laughed. He had a laugh with no smile in it. "We'll cut it," he said.

When they came up I'd been standing over the coffee pot

with a fresh-filled cup. Now I stepped a little away from the fire, still holding the cup. "I don't think so," I said.

Bowers turned to look at me. He turned his head straight around and looked at me out of both eyes, the way a snake does. He had his gun tied down, and it was a Bisley Colt. I remember there was a patch on his vest, sewn with lighter material. The patch was below the heart.

"We've got twenty-five fighting men," he said, and he was measuring me. "We'll cut it, all right."

"You don't need twenty-five," I said, stepping out a bit more from the fire. "You only need one if he's good enough. Otherwise twenty-five couldn't do it, nor fifty. The boys here," I added, "like a fight. Ain't had much fun this trip."

He kept looking at me. Mustang Roberts was off on my right. He had his leg bandaged but there was nothing wrong with his gun hand. Kid Beaton was a little farther over.

"Who're you?" he asked softly.

"My name is Ryan Tyler," I said, "and I own some of these cows."

Leet Bowers's eyes glinted and his tongue touched his lips. He was laughing a little now. "Rye Tyler," he said, "who killed Rice Wheeler and then let Burdette run him out of Colorado."

It was poor shooting light, with only the fire flickering, and the shadows uncertain and strange.

"Burdette never ran me out of anywhere," I said, "but that's no matter. You ain't cutting this herd."

"Burdette ran you out of Colorado," he repeated, a taunt in his tone. "You're yellow!"

My first bullet cut the top of that white patch on his vest, my second notched the bottom of the hole made by the first.

Leet Bowers fell with his head in the fire but he didn't feel it. He was dead.

It happened so fast that nobody had a chance to do anything, but no sooner had the sound of the shots died than Kid Beaton threw down on them with his Sharps. "You boys drag it," he said, and gesturing toward the body, "Take that with you."

"Now," said the cook. He was holding one of those old Colt revolving shotguns. "Or we can bury all of you here."

They dragged Leet Bowers out of the fire and slung him over his saddle. None of them looked so very spry and I'd say they'd lost some wind.

Bennett walked toward them. "Don't come near my herd. If so much as one cow is missing, we'll hunt down every man jack of you and hang you to the highest tree. And if there isn't a tree, we'll drag you."

They rode off, drifting mighty quiet.

Mustang Roberts looked around at me, drinking coffee. "See that? With his left hand, yet. And never spilled his coffee!"

Bennett turned around to me. "Nice work, Tyler. I've heard of this man. He killed a rider two months ago and since then has had everything his own way."

For once I didn't feel bad about a shooting. In Leet Bowers's eyes there had been something vicious. The flat, mean look of a man who kills and wants to kill.

Outside of Wichita, bunching the herd, Roberts rode over to me. "Goin' back to Colorado?"

"Uh-huh."

"Who's this Burdette? Heard something of him?"

"Gunman. Mighty salty, they say."

"Have trouble?"

"Words." I headed a steer back into the herd. "He had his chance."

"Seems he's talkin'."

"Well," I said, "I'm not hunting trouble. But I am agoing back."

"Maybe I'll ride along."

"Welcome."

In Wichita Bennett decided to hold his herd for a better price, and advised me to do the same. "It's down from what it's been, but there's only a few cows around and no herd within miles. The price will go up."

"I'm selling," I told him. "I want to go to Colorado."

He nodded, chewing on an unlighted cigar. Then he took the cigar from his lips and looked at it. "You stay with me," he said. "We'll make a good thing of this, then bring another herd from Texas. A few years and you'll be a rich man."

"Maybe. . . . I don't want to kill a man for every herd, though."

"Won't have to." He gestured south. "By now every herd cutter on the trail knows what happened to Leet Bowers. There'll be no more trouble."

It was there for me. And I liked cattle drives. It was hard, brutal work, but it was strong work, and good work, and a man was doing things. There was talk of taking cattle to Wyoming and Montana, and there was open country up there. New country, fresh country.

But there was a girl in Colorado I kept thinking about. She had been only a youngster then, but by now . . .

"No," I told him. "Thanks anyway. I'm going back."

"Burdette?"

"No. I hope I never see him. It's . . . well, there's somebody there I want to see. And there's that ranch I want."

Two days later I sold for a nice price and left there with more than seven thousand dollars. Some I carried in gold, some in a draft on a St. Louis bank. Mustang Roberts rode along with me.

It was late fall, the air turning crisp and sharp. I liked the feel of it because it reminded me of the high country. We rode west, heading for Dodge.

The new town was at the end of the tracks, and crowded with hide hunters, the buffalo men of the plains country. We crowded up to the bar for a drink, something I rarely did, but I wanted to see how things went in this wild town.

The first person I saw was Billy Dixon, whom I'd known in Kansas City.

"Come with me," he argued. "I'm going out west of here and shoot in the big herd. We can make a fortune in a few months."

"Not me. I don't like to kill."

Dixon glanced at me. I guess Mustang Roberts did, too. My face started getting red, and I told them, "I mean that. I kill for food or if somebody pushes me. Not otherwise."

"Reminds me," Dixon said. "Billy Ogg told me that gambler we knew, that Charley Woods—Billy said he was killed."

"That so?"

"Must have happened when you were in New Orleans. Chris Lillie was telling the story around that Woods tried to murder some Western man."

"Probably deserved what he got."

I wasn't telling anybody anything. Four men I'd killed now, not counting Indians. It was nothing to be proud of. Nobody but a tinhorn ever scratched notches on his gun, and I never would.

Nor was I wanting to be known as a killer. So far nobody knew about Jack McGarry. That is, it was known in California, but there wasn't too much traffic between the cow and mining camps. The bad men of one group weren't much known to the other.

So far as the public was concerned, I had killed but two men—Rice Wheeler and Leet Bowers. So far, not so many knew about me, although the reputation of the two I'd killed had been such as to make folks believe me a dangerous man.

No man in his right mind wanted such a reputation, which immediately made a man a target for half the would-be gun slingers in the country. And if I were to be known for something, I wanted it to be something of which I could be proud.

"Thinking about you the other day," Dixon continued. "Didn't you tell me you worked for a man named Hetrick? Out in Mason Crossing, Colorado?"

"Uh-huh. Fine man."

"Then you'll be sorry to hear this, but you'd better know it now. He's dead. Ollie Burdette killed him."

TEN

It took a while for it to sink in. Hetrick almost never carried a gun, and he was a man who never got angry with anybody. He did not believe in killing. He was a stern but gentle man. Yet he was also a man who would not compromise his principles.

Even so, there seemed no way he could have come to trouble with Burdette. He was rarely in town, and he did not loaf when he was there, or drink. He did what business brought him there and left. He was a man who preferred his own family, his own home.

Then I began to think. Hetrick had stood beside me when I made Burdette take water.

To Burdette it would be a galling thing to know that even one man lived who had seen him back down, who had seen him refuse an issue.

That must have been it. Burdette could not rest easy as long as one man knew. And it might even be that Hetrick had heard Burdette's story of running me out of the state and had told the true version of what happened that day on the street.

A thing like that would ride Burdette. His reputation as a dangerous man was all he had. He was an empty man. But he was a killer.

"When did it happen?"

"Four, five months ago."

"I see."

The glass in my fingers still held whisky. I had never cared for it, and suddenly I cared less for it now. Right now I had only one idea: I was going back to Mason Crossing.

Yet it was not Ollie Burdette that I thought of, it was Liza. What about Liza? Where would that leave her?

"You like this town?" I asked Mustang.

"I lost nothing here."

"All right. We're riding."

Billy Dixon went out on the walk and watched us get in the saddle. "You take care of yourself," he warned. "That Burdette's a bad man."

Me, I just waved a hand.

Country slid away behind us. Big, open, grassy, wonderful country. Two days out we saw the big herd, black sea of shifting buffalo as far as the eye could reach. Never saw anything like it. Made my gray plumb skittish, but we circled and come sundown we followed a stream bed through the herd and away.

Country began to get rougher, all cut up with ravines and some high mesas. I was getting so I liked the smell of buffalo-chip fires, although it brought back memories of Pap and the wagon train.

Someday I wanted to go back and find his grave and put a stone marker on it. He would have liked that. But I wouldn't move him. He was always one to say, "let the chips fall where they may." He had fallen there, and he would like to lie there, right in the middle of the West. He could have built himself a good life, Pap could. Sometimes I wondered what would have become of me if he had lived. Probably I'd never have used a gun. I'd have gone to school to be a lawyer or something. A man never knows.

Bennett had tried to tell me one night before I left Wichita that men like me were needed, that the country had to grow up, and it had growing pains, and that all the guns must not be on the bad side. There had to be guns for the right, too.

That I knew. Yet it was a hard thing to be sure one was always on the right, and sometimes there wasn't a chance for figuring out the right and wrong of it when guns started smoking.

We rode on, into rougher, wilder country. One time we had a brush with Comanches. Nobody killed. Mustang downed one of their horses a quarter of a mile away with his Sharps. They didn't figure to like that sort of shootin' and they went to hellin' across the country.

"Never forget you saved my bacon that time," Mustang said, shoving a shell into the breech.

"What time?"

"Them Kiowas. They had me, cold turkey. Horse dead, bullet in my leg, and just three rounds of ammunition left. Then you come arunnin'. Mighty fine sight you made."

"You was late for supper."

Mite of snow came time and again. The country was high now, the weather crisp, the nights cold. There was more brown than green in the grass now, and the cottonwoods looked like tall feathers of gold with their yellow leaves. In the morning there was fog in the low ground, and sometimes it was noon before a man rightly began to feel warmth in the air.

The gray was growing his winter coat. He didn't look so pretty any more, but mighty ragged and tough. He was all horse, that one.

This was a man's country—wide open, big as all creation, and as far as you could look, nothing but rolling miles. Antelope bounded up and away, giving queer jumps. Sometimes a rabbit scurried out of the way, and at night there were coyotes calling the moon.

Once we sighted an Army patrol and went out of our way to get some tobacco and talk a bit. It was a routine patrol. Somebody had seen some Cheyennes, but they turned out to be Shawnees, peaceful, hunting buffalo from the fringe of a small herd.

"We goin' to Denver?" Mustang wanted to know.

"Uh-huh."

"I want to get me a sheep coat. This here wind cuts a man."

All I could think of was Burdette, shooting Hetrick. Time a man like that was sent packing.

I wasn't going to kill him. I was going to do worse. I was going to break him. I was going to bust him right in front of people. I was going to ruin him as a gunman.

The one thing a gunman can't stand is to lose face. Too many men hunting them. Too many men wanting to make a cheap kill. Once they get shown up, it's only a matter of time until they are killed . . . unless they leave the country.

We reached Denver in late September with snow sifting out of a lead-gray sky. We reached Denver and headed for a hotel. I had money, so we went to the best.

That night I lay in bed thinking, staring wide awake at the ceiling. What did a man come to? Where could a man get, drifting like this? I had a little stake now, and the thing to do was to go someplace and light. Get some roots down. Maybe I should marry.

That thought stopped me a bit. I didn't like to think of being tied down. Not when I might have to ride on at any time. But Logan Pollard had stopped. Good old Logan! I'd sure like to see him. I told myself that and it was true. By now they probably had a family. No time at all since I'd seen them, but it seemed a long while. I was going to be twenty soon, and I'd been through the mill.

Getting up, I went to the washbowl and poured some water and bathed my face. I picked up a towel and dried it and looked at myself in the mirror.

Ryan Tyler, I told myself, there you are. What looked at me was a smooth brown face without any mustache, curly hair brushed back from the forehead, but always inclined to fall over it. A brown face that had strong cheekbones, and a strong jaw, but the eyes were sort of green and there wasn't any smile around the mouth.

That wasn't good. A man should smile. And there was something a little cold around the eyes. Was I cold? I didn't feel cold inside. Not a bit.

Never had many friends, but then, I'd drifted too much, and the few friends I'd had were good ones. Logan Pollard, Hetrick, and now Mustang Roberts. Yes, and Billy Dixon, Ogg, and Bennett. Good men they were, all of them.

But where did that leave me? The one thing I could do better than most men was the one thing I did not want to do. Maybe, as Bennett had said, the West needed its gun fighters. Maybe in a land where there was no law, some restraint was needed for the lawless. But I didn't want to be one of them.

What did it get a man, twenty years old and no smile? Twenty years, and four dead men behind him, and eyes that were always a little cool, a little remote, a little watchful. I wanted no more of it. I wanted to get away, to make an end of it.

But a man does what he has to do. That's why a man is a man.

I walked back and got into bed and tried to sleep. When it was daybreak I did sleep for an hour or so.

Outside the ground was two feet deep in snow. In the streets men were shoveling walks, their breath smoky in the cold air. It was no time to travel, but it was no time to stop, either.

"Hetrick's been dead a few months," Roberts argued. "Take your time. Burdette ain't going nowhere. If he does, maybe so much the better."

That made sense, and crossing those mountains in the winter would be no picnic. Even if a man made it, and the old-timers were smart enough not to try.

Denver was booming those days and gambling was booming right along with it. Maybe I'd played poker a mite, but I was no gambling man. Just the same, those places were wide open and mighty exciting. Maybe, too, it was because I was still just a boy, although I'd been caring for myself for a long time now.

So Mustang and me, we made them all. The Morgue, the

Bucket of Blood, the Palace, the Chicken Coop, and Murphy's Exchange. All of them wide open. Crowded, too.

Soapy Smith was there, a fellow we were to hear a lot about later. Young Bat Masterson was in town, and Doc Halliday drifted through, bound for Texas. Kit Carson was there for some time, and one of the Bents from down New Mexico way.

One night after we got back to the hotel Mustang and me were having supper when he nudged me.

"Rye, there's a dude got his eye on you. He's been studying you for some time now. You ain't been in no trouble back East, have you?"

Mustang, he was a blond fellow with a lean, tough face. No gun slinger, but a mean man to face in a fight, and game as they come. He was also a man very sharp to notice things, so when I could, I glanced around.

This tenderfoot sat across the room. He was a tall man with black hair, gray at the temples, and mighty handsome. Maybe he was fifty years old, but dressed real fine. When I looked around he saw me and our eyes held for a moment, and then he got up and started across the room.

I wasn't duded up as I had been in New Orleans. My fancy clothes were all packed away. Nonetheless, I didn't look so bad, I guess. I had on those black calfskin boots, a gray wool shirt with a black string tie, and a black, braided short coat that I'd picked up in Texas. It was cut Mexican style. And I had on my gray pants, tucked into my boots.

Without looking again, I tried to place the stranger. He might be a gambler, but somehow that didn't fit, either. And at a quick glance my guess was that he wasn't packing a gun.

He paused alongside the table. "I beg your pardon. My name is Denison Mead."

I got up. "I'm Ryan Tyler," I said, "and this here's Mustang Roberts. Will you sit down?"

"Thank you." He sat down and motioned for his bottle of wine to be brought to our table. "I'm a lawyer," he said, "representing a mining company. I've been looking over some gold properties."

"Sounds prosperous. I've been dealing in cows."

"Texas?"

"Lately."

We talked a mite, just casual conversation. He had nothing to say about his reason for joining us. He was pleasant enough, yet I had an idea he was fishing for something, something he wanted to know. He didn't ask many questions, but he had a way of getting a man to talk. But I hadn't played poker for nothing. I wasn't going to tell him anything more than I wanted to. On the other hand, I'd nothing to conceal.

"This country your home? Or is it Texas?"

"I'm drifting," I said. "No home, properly speaking, but I aim to get a little home over in the mountains. A ranch, I've got in mind."

He looked at me thoughtfully. "About twenty? Or twenty-one?"

"Twenty," I said.

We talked some of cattle, and he gathered I'd recently been in Kansas City and New Orleans.

"Were you born out here?"

It came quickly, but it slid into the conversation in such a way that I became suspicious. Something about the way he said it made me believe this was what he had been planning to ask all the time.

I was getting uneasy. That shooting in New Orleans, now. That was off my home grounds, and they looked at things different there than out here. Unless somebody had stolen the gun, they would have found Woods with a pistol in his hand, but no telling what Chris Lillie might tell the law. Still, he was apt to tell them nothing. Not his kind.

"No, sir," I said finally, "I was born in Maryland. Or so my pap told me. Lived in New York when I was a boy, then in Missouri and Kansas."

"You've traveled a good bit." He paused, and me, I'm good at reading sign. I can read it on faces as well as on the ground, and that's why I play a fair game of poker. And right then I had a feeling this was another question he'd been building up to.

"You've no home," he said. "Wouldn't you say your home was where your parents were?"

"Ma died on the way West," I explained. "Pap was killed by Indians when I was twelve."

"So. I've heard of such stories," he commented. "I guess they're a part of the West. Men have to die to build any country strong. All of them don't die in battle, though."

"Pap did," I said, and then I told him about it. Mustang had never heard the story, either, but he heard it now. How Ma took sick and didn't really have no decent care, though Pap did the best he could. Then she died and when she was buried we started on West. I told him all that, and I told him about the last few hours, about the wagon train leaving us, about the fight in the ravine. But I didn't tell them about what I did to the Indians, or about Jack McGarry.

He was a pleasant man, easy to talk to, and he was friendly. I told him about Logan Pollard, and about reading Plutarch.

"And did you read it five times?"

"Only four, so far. But I'll get to it."

"And this place you're going to . . . Mason Crossing? Do you intend to stay there for a while?"

"Prob'ly," I said, "but I might move on."

After he left us I did some thinking about it. No law that I knew about was looking for me. Woods was killed in self-defense, and he was no account, anyway. Those days, men like him didn't attract much notice when they died. Everybody figured the country was saved a hanging. Nevertheless, this talk worried me some.

Tired of hanging around gambling joints, I bought a dozen books and lay on my bed in my room through the long cold days and read. Outside the wind blew a lot, and every other day or so it snowed. All the passes were closed and nobody was traveling. The streets sounded with the jingle of sleigh bells and the stoves in the saloons glowed cherry red.

At night sometimes we sat around a big stove in the lobby and yarned. I didn't talk much, but I liked to listen. There were mining men and cattlemen there, gamblers, drifters, and businessmen. There were drummers and cattle buyers, and men just looking for something to put money into. Most of them had been around a lot and they talked well.

Up in my room I read a couple of books by an English writer named Dickens, and I read the *Scarlet Letter*, by Hawthorne. There was some poetry, too, by an English writer named Byron. This I liked a mighty lot.

One day when I came back to the hotel that lawyer was waiting for me. Mustang was out somewhere, but this fellow was sitting in a big leather chair in the almost empty lobby.

He seemed anxious to talk private, so we went upstairs, and when my room door was closed, he turned on me. "Tyler, I've been hearing some talk. Don't go back to Mason Crossing."

This stopped me flat-footed, but I waited a long minute and then said, "Why not?" And I was pretty cool, for I want no stranger butting into my affairs.

"Burdette will kill you."

"I doubt it. Anyway," I looked him right in the eye, "I'm going back."

He said no more about that, walking up and down the room a couple of times. Then suddenly he stopped and looked at me. "How many men have you actually killed, Tyler?"

"None of your business."

He looked at me for a long time, his eyes sort of searching my face. Yet there was something friendly about it all, and something worried, too. Almost as if he had an interest.

"Of course," he agreed finally, "you're right. It is none of my business. Only . . . well, no matter."

He crossed to the door. "Whatever you do, take care of yourself. And you may hear from me."

He went out and the next day I heard he had taken the stage for Cheyenne. Nobody in town knew much about him except that he had been investigating the titles to some mining claims, and he had looked over some prospects. At least, looked them over as much as he could with the weather what it was.

Two days later the cold spell broke and I shook Mustang out of a sleep.

"Pack up, man. We're riding."

He didn't argue any. I expect town was getting on his nerves, too. Anyway, within the hour we were riding out of town, headed west.

The route we had taken swung south by way of Durango, and as the thaw was on, we made good time.

We reached Durango late at night and the next morning I found a squaw who had been making buckskin breeches, and I bought some. I was beginning to feel as if I belonged again.

This was my country. I liked the largeness of it, the space, the sharp, clear mountain air, and the riding. When I had a ranch it was going to be a horse ranch.

While we rode west I told Mustang about this Denison Mead, and what he had said about staying away from Mason Crossing.

"Mighty good advice," Roberts agreed, "but what's he takin' on so about?"

"Can't figure that—unless he knows Burdette."

"Ain't that. But he was askin' a lot of questions about you."

We forgot about that during the day, for we were coming up to my old country again, and somewhere ahead was the ranch, and I'd be seeing Liza again. To say nothing of Old Blue. And Mrs. Hetrick was almost like my own mother. It had been a long time. Too long. And Hetrick was dead.

Those last few miles before we reached the ranch sure fretted me. Finally I started the gray into a trot, and Mustang, he came right along with me. When the town came in sight I cut around back of it toward the ranch. I could hardly wait to see the place, and to see Mrs. Hetrick and Liza.

The gray was almost at a run when I rounded to the gate. We went through, and then I pulled up.

Grass grew in the dooryard and there were tumbleweeds

against the fence. The porch was sagging and the door banged on loose hinges. A low wind moaned among the pines and around the eaves, and I stood there looking around, a big empty feeling inside me.

I got down from the saddle and walked slowly through the house. She was empty. The folks were gone, and from the look of things, they had been gone for a long time.

Inside I felt as empty as the house, and when a long wind with a touch of snow on it came down off the mountain, I shivered. The gate at the garden creaked and banged, and I stood there, sick and empty. Liza was gone.

ELEVEN

The Crossing was built up some. I could see that as we rounded into the main street. It was built up, and Mason's Store was bigger. There was a long awning in front of the rooming house and it had become a two-story hotel.

Thinking suddenly, I turned aside and rode around to the cemetery. Mustang, he trailed along, never leaving me.

At the cemetery gate I got down and went in. It was like so many of those Western cemeteries, a high knoll outside of town with the wind blowing across it and tumbleweeds racked against the fences.

And I found what I was looking for, and more. Hetrick's grave, and beside it the grave of his wife, who had died just four months later.

Both gone.

And Liza? She might still be in town, although somehow I was sure she wasn't.

"Mustang," I said, "I got to get me a man. But I don't aim to kill him, not unless I have to. I want you to go down to town. You be careful, because this Burdette is mighty mean. But you listen around and find out if he's still there, and where he is. I want to come on him unexpected-like. I want to get the jump."

Sitting under some cedars there by the graveyard, with the gray grass alongside me, I waited. Maybe I slept some. Any-

93

way, lights were coming on in town before Mustang came back.

The chill had awakened me, and when I sat up I heard his horse. He rode up to the gate and got down, then he walked over and squatted on his heels and began to build a smoke.

"Burdette's there, all right. Mighty mean, like you say. The folks got no use for him, but he's still marshal and they're scared. Ever' night about this time he makes his rounds. Then he goes to the saloon and sits until everybody turns in. He makes another round, then he turns in himself.

"Come morning, he goes up to the restaurant for breakfast, and he sits around some. He killed another man about two weeks ago, and I got an idea the town would like to get shut of him."

"You eat?"

"Uh-huh."

"I ain't hungry. I think we'd best bed down right here. I want to get him in the morning at breakfast."

"Good. The restaurant has a back door, too. You want I should come in and get the drop?"

"No. You leave it alone unless somebody tries to butt in. This is my branding. I'll heat my own irons and make my own mark."

When we were all rolled up in our blankets and lying there listening to the town sounds, he said, all of a sudden, "That girl? Liza Hetrick? She left town six, seven months ago. And she only had sixty-three dollars. Took the stage out. West."

"You should have been a Pinkerton."

Mustang drew on his cigarette. "Maybe I will be." He chuckled. "But first we find your gal."

Morning found us with our beds rolled and ready. We took the trail down into town and went through streets and alleys until Mustang could show me the back door to the restaurant. Then we rode past it.

"We may have to leave fast," I said.

Mustang chuckled dryly. "You leave. I'll be right behind you, maybe ahead of you."

We got down and tied our horses and went inside. Mustang went through the door first with me right behind him, my head down.

There were four people in the restaurant: the woman who ran it, old Mason, who sat at a table alone, and two cow hands in from the forks of the creek.

Four people besides Burdette. He was sitting behind a table facing the door.

When we got three steps inside the door Mustang side-stepped and I was looking into those mean, slate-gray eyes of Ollie Burdette's.

He was surprised. That was plain. And he never got a chance to get over it. I walked right up to his table because he didn't like it close up. I walked right up, and I had only two steps to make to get there, and then I spoke up, loud and clear.

"Burdette, you murdered Hetrick. That old man never packed a gun in his life. And you told it around that you had run me out of town. That's why you killed him, because he knew you were a liar. He saw you take water that time."

He hadn't no time to get his mouth open. Me, I just kept shoving it at him, and when he started to drop his hand, I slammed against the table and smashed him back against the wall. And then I slapped him twice across the mouth, once with each hand.

Suddenly I was mad. I was mad clean through, but not killing mad. I just wanted to destroy everything he was or thought he was.

It had been a complete surprise, shocking to Ollie Burdette, and my lunge against the table had pinned his gun holster.

But suddenly I jerked the table away and stepped in. He grabbed for his gun, but I hit him. He staggered and I swung a boot from the floor and kicked his gun loose. It fell, and as he grabbed for it, I hit him in the face.

He put his hands up and rushed at me, but he was a man

who had trusted to guns. Big as he was—and he was heavier than me—he was no fighter. I hit him in the belly, then on the side of the face. That last blow cut deep and knocked him around, smashing his head against the edge of the table.

He got no chance at all from me. No more than he had given some of the men he killed. I grabbed him by the collar and back-walked him to the door, slapping him across the face at every step. Then I shoved him out of the door and into the street.

He fell in the dust, and fell hard. Then he lunged to his feet, but he didn't know which way to turn. He was caught without a gun, and without a gun he was nothing. He started to back up, and I went after him.

Walking him back across the street, I slapped him. He tried to fight back, striking at me, trying to knock my hands down. A time or two he hit me, but he had been sitting around taking it easy while I had been riding, working, roughing it.

In front of the saloon, with fifty men looking on, I knocked him down. He got up and rushed me, and I hit him in the mouth, smashing his lips into his teeth. He backed up, bloody and beaten. I walked up to him and, throwing one from the hip, knocked him down again. Then I picked him up and tossed him bodily into the water trough. Then I fished him out and stood him up against it.

"You murdered Hetrick. You might as well have murdered his wife. You bragged around that you run me out. You're just a two-bit bad man in a four-bit town."

He couldn't talk. His wind was gone and his mouth was all blood and torn lips.

"You got a horse?" I looked around at Old Man Mason, who had followed us. "Where's his horse?"

"I'll get it." The voice was familiar, and I looked around. It was Kipp.

Burdette stood there, soaked to the hide and shivering. He shook his head like a wounded bear. It had all happened so fast that he hadn't no time to get set for it. Right then I don't think he had realized yet what was happening to him. Too long he had lorded it around, doing it all on the strength of his gun. And now he had no gun.

When Kipp came up with the horse, I told Burdette to get into the saddle. "Now ride. And don't stop riding until the week is gone."

"I got property," he protested, able to talk at last. "I got stuff at the house."

"You lose it," I said, "like Hetrick lost his ranch."

He stared at me, and those poison-mean eyes were shocked and dull. "Don't I get a gun? Without a gun my life ain't worth a plugged nickel."

"No more than the lives of some of those you killed. You get no gun."

He never said anything more. He just walked his horse off down the street and out of town. Somebody gave a halfhearted cheer, but not much of one. Trouble was, they were shocked, too.

"Kipp," I said, "where'd Liza go?"

"Don't know, Rye. She wouldn't take any help. After her ma died she aimed to take care of herself. She didn't get much out of the ranch. After Hetrick was killed, the horse thieves stole them blind. All I know is, she bought a ticket for Alta. She would have had about forty dollars left when she got there."

Mustang and me, we mounted up and rode out of town that night. There was nothing at the Crossing for me now, and Mustang, he just seemed to want to stay along with me. And no man had a better friend.

We never talked any about being partners. We never said much of anything to each other. We just rode together and shared together, and that was the way of it.

Alta was a boom mining town, half across the state of Utah. It wasn't a Mormon town, being populated mostly by gentile miners from Nevada or Colorado. Many had been working on the Comstock Lode and some had come down from Alder Gulch, Montana.

I'd been hearing about Alta. It was a sure-enough mean town, where they killed men every night and mostly every day. The mines were rich and the town was booming. It was wide open and ararin'.

Never before had I had much of any place to go, or any purpose in life. Now I had one. I was going to find Liza. I was going to make sure she was doing all right. It wasn't right for a girl of seventeen to be traipsing around rough country on her own. No telling what had happened to her.

Right then I thought some mighty fierce thoughts, and I angered up some, just thinking things that might have happened to her.

It was snowing when we rode into town and stabled our horses. The first thing to do was to find a place to sleep, but I left that to Mustang and started for a saloon.

The saloon was the club, the meeting place, the clearing house for information. In a mining camp or a cow town the same rule held true, and often enough the company would include many who drink little or nothing at all.

The snow was falling fast, and except in the street, churned into mud by the passing of men, horses, and heavy wagons, the ground rapidly grew white. Huge ore wagons dragged by, their shouting drivers bundled up against the cold, their huge horses or oxen leaning into the harness as they strained against great loads.

A music box was going up the street, and in the feeble light of a lantern behind a saloon a man was splitting wood.

When I pushed open the door of the Bucket of Blood I was met by a wave of hot air, thick with tobacco smoke and the sour odor of bad whisky. At least a hundred men crowded the small room, standing three deep at the bar. Bearded men loafed along the walls, leaning or squatting and watching for a favorable moment to grab a chair.

This was a familiar scene, and I had known it before, in other towns. There were even familiar faces, men whose names I didn't know, but whom I had seen in Denver, Santa Fe, or Mason Crossing. There was even one I knew from New Orleans.

Moving through the crowd, I was lucky enough to get close to the bar. Beside me two men talked Norwegian, and down the bar I heard a man order in German, and the bartender replied in the same language. This was the West, a melting pot, a conglomeration. These were hard, tough, reckless men from all over the world, following the lure of a wild new country and quick riches in the mines.

No telling what had happened to Liza here. Maybe she had seen the place and what it was like and had gone on. Certainly this town was no place for a pretty girl alone.

Two hours later I was no closer to finding her. True, I wasn't asking questions. I was listening, drifting from place to place, keeping my eyes open. The stage station was closed, so I couldn't check there.

Snow kept falling. The Gold Miner's Daughter was jammed when Mustang found me there.

"Got a place," he said, "and it wasn't easy. This town is crowded."

We drifted around the tables. We had a drink, and I played a little roulette and lost fifteen dollars, then won five of it back.

Turning toward the door, I saw a man stop and take another look at me, then walk on. He knew me from somewhere.

All of a sudden, somebody swore, men jammed back out of the way, and a gun blasted.

It was that quick, and all over. A man in digging clothes was backing up slowly, both hands holding his stomach. He sat down and rolled over, moaning softly.

The gambler with the gun in his hand walked around the table and stood over him. Coolly he lifted his pistol for another shot.

Me, I don't know why I did it, but I stepped from the crowd.

"He's dying. Leave him alone."

The gambler was in his shirt sleeves and vest. He was a tall, pale man with a mustache. His eyes held such cruelty as I've never seen before. He looked coolly at me.

"You're making it your business?"

He held a derringer in his hand. It was one of those short guns with two barrels, each holding a .44 cartridge.

"I am."

He looked at me. His gun was in his hand, half lifted. Mine was in my holster. Yet he had one shot left, and if he did not kill me with that shot, he was a dead man.

He shrugged. "He'll die, anyway. No use to shoot again."

The man on the floor coughed heavily and stared at the gambler. "Cheat . . . You cheat . . ." and then he sagged back on the floor and died.

He wore a gun, all right, but it was buttoned under his coat. He'd had no chance at all.

"He lies," the gambler said contemptuously. "He just couldn't take losing."

"He sure didn't have that gun where he could use it," I said.

The gambler was turning away, but now he swung around to face me, his face livid. "You keep your mouth shut!" he shouted. "I've taken all I'm going to."

"If I was the law in this town," I said, "you'd be on the first stage out. And you'd never show your face in town again. This was murder. He had no chance, none at all."

The derringer started to lift, coming up slowly. And just when I was going to take my chance and draw, I heard Mustang's voice.

"His gun ain't drawed, mister . . . but mine is!"

And it was. The gambler didn't like that big six looking at him. He shrugged and turned sharply away.

"You push your luck, stranger," a miner said quietly. "That's Key Novak. He's killed three men in the past two months."

With Mustang at my side I turned away and walked out, leaving the Gold Miner's Daughter and starting up the street. We had taken only a few steps when a door closed behind us and we heard footsteps on the walk.

Flattening into a doorway with my gun in my hand, I watched three men coming down the walk. Mustang was standing on the other side, half behind a water trough and an awning post. A frozen water barrel offered added protection.

The men drew abreast and in the light from a nearby window I recognized the man who had appeared to recognize me in the saloon. They stopped, and this man spoke. "Tyler, you don't know me, but I used to see you around Kansas City. Heard about you from Billy Dixon."

"So?"

"I heard you were the man who killed Rice Wheeler? And Leet Bowers?"

"That's right."

"Tyler, we want a marshal in this town. One who will clean out the crooked gamblers and the thugs. We had two knife killings last night. We don't know who did them. We had a miner killed last week. The crooks are running the town. We'll give you two hundred and fifty a month to clean up for us."

This was a surprise. I'd never fancied myself as the law before. On the other hand, there would be no better way to look the town over for Liza.

"All right," I said, "but I want Mustang as deputy."

"As you like." He hesitated. "My name is Murdock. I own the general store. This is Eph Graham, agent for Wells Fargo. Newton here has the hardware store and the mining supplies. We're the town council."

"All right."

"One thing . . . the present marshal is John Lang. He's the Texas gunman. He has to be fired."

My eyes went over the three of them. A wagon was passing in the street and the clop-clop of the heavy hoofs in the stiffening mud was loud. "I fire him?" I asked. Newton looked uneasy, and Murdock shifted his feet, but Graham nodded.

"He's dangerous . . . and we think he's with the crooks."

Gesturing toward the crowded saloons, I said, "This won't be easy. Suppose somebody gets hurt?"

"We'll back you. Organize vigilantes if you want them."

"We won't need them."

Murdock took some badges from his pocket and handed them to me. I shook my head. "These are all right, but I want a signed paper, appointing us. Signed by all three of you."

They gave it to me and I was the new marshal of Alta, with Mustang Roberts as deputy.

They walked away and we stood there getting used to the idea. Mustang, he looked over at me and grinned. "Like 'em tough, don't you?" Then he added, "Now we can really look for your girl."

"What I was figuring," I said, "so let's get busy."

He hitched his guns. "What's first?"

"We fire the marshal. Rather, I fire him. You stand by."

So we turned around and walked down the street toward the marshal's office and I was glad Mustang Roberts walked beside me.

TWELVE

It was a square frame building in front of the stone jail. It had two rooms: the outer office, and an inner room where the marshal slept.

John Lang was sitting behind the desk with his feet on it, and there was another man, a bearded man, who sat on an iron safe against the wall.

The floor was dirty, a few scattered cigar and cigarette butts lying around, and some old papers, flyspecked and yellow. There was a rack holding several rifles and shotguns.

Pushing the door open, I stepped in. Lang looked up at me, then looked again. He saw that badge on my shirt and his face set and his eyes grew wary.

"Who're you?"

"The new marshal. I'm to tell you you're fired."

The bearded man chuckled. "You git out'n here, kid, whilst you're able. Ain't nobody firin' us. They done tried. Ain't they, Hal?"

With some people you don't talk, you don't explain. I'd told 'em; now it was up to me to fire 'em.

Before Lang knew what was happening, I grabbed the boots on the desk and slammed them to the floor. His boots hit the floor and he came up with a lunge, but the advantage was mine, and I kept it. As he clawed for his gun I hit him in the

103

mouth and he sat back down in the chair so hard it toppled over backward.

It happened so fast the deputy scarcely got his mouth open, and he had just started to move when I turned with the punch and hit him in the teeth, slamming his skull against the wall with a dull thud.

He was stunned when Mustang grabbed him. As I swung back, Lang's gun was coming free. So I palmed mine and shot him. He took the first bullet in the throat and the second in the chest, and he just lay back on the floor and stayed there.

Then I turned on the deputy, whom Mustang had disarmed. "You're fired, too. You want to take a chance and draw, or do you want to get out of town?"

He wanted to draw but he didn't want to die. He stared hard at me, sweating it out for a full minute, and then he said, "Soon's the storm's over I'll ride."

"You'll ride now. Storm or no storm. If you're in town an hour from now, you can die or go to jail."

He swallowed, backing off. "Wait'll you hear from Billings! You won't get away with this! Why, he'll break you! He'll break that damn town council, too."

So I hit him again. "Beat it," I said, and he beat it.

Mustang, who had been holding the deputy's gun, ready to return it if he decided to gamble, put it in a desk drawer.

He took out the makings and rolled a smoke. "You know," he said, "when you first joined up back there in Texas, some of the boys thought you were a sure-enough tenderfoot. They should have seen what I seen."

I looked around the dirty little office. It was nothing that would make a man respect the law. I looked over at Roberts. "You, you're my deputy. We enforce the law. We enforce it tough. We don't shoot anybody unless we have to, we don't hit anybody unless we have to. But we only give an order once.

"No card cheating. No robbery. No burglary. No robbing drunks. No beating up innocent people. No gun fights. No women molested."

"Fist fights?"

"As long as they don't bust up property. If the match looks pretty even, let 'em have it out. If it gets one-sided, stop it.

"We protect the helpless, the innocent, and the folks who are doing legitimate business."

"All right." He glanced at Lang's body. "I guess I better get him out of here."

"No. We'll let Billings do that."

"Who?"

"Billings. From what the deputy said, he figures he's boss. We'll let him take Lang out and dig the grave. We'll let him mop up the floor."

Mustang Roberts drew a deep breath. He looked at me to see if I was serious, but he needn't have. He'd known me long enough to know I didn't talk idle.

"This will be something to see." He hesitated. "I ain't told you before, but this here Billings may know something about your girl."

That stopped me. I felt myself getting sick inside. In town only a few hours, I'd heard enough to know that Billings ran the houses where the red-light women were. I knew he ran two of the toughest saloons. Men leaving those saloons with money seldom got far.

"Don't get me wrong," Mustang added. "It's nothing definite. Only he was seen talking to her, and he was taking a powerful interest in her. That was right after she got off the stage."

"All right. First things first. We'll let Billings bury his dead."

Billings was a big man. He was a man with black, plastered-down hair on a round skull, a wide face, florid of complexion, and a black walrus mustache, but trimmed more neatly than most. He stood about three inches over six feet, and he must have weighed well over two hundred pounds. He wore a striped silk shirt with sleeve garters and black pants. He smoked a big black cigar and he carried his gun in a holster shoved down in his waistband. It was good for a fast draw.

His place was smaller than some and dirtier than most, but there were a dozen games going when we pushed through the door bringing a blast of cold, fresh air into the stuffy interior. I walked over to him. "Billings?"

He turned to look at me and his eyes dropped to the badge, then lifted. "You show that to John Lang?"

"Yes." I spoke quietly. "It was the last thing he ever saw."

You could have heard a feather drop in that room. You couldn't hear a breath drawn. The idea was beginning to work its way through their heads. That Texas gunman was gone. John Lang was dead.

Mustang Roberts was obviously another Texan. About me, they didn't know. They were going to learn fast.

Billings took the cigar from his teeth. "I see. Let's go into my office and have a talk."

"We haven't time. Lang is lying on the floor in my office and he needs burying. Also, the floor needs mopping."

He looked at me, his hard pale-blue eyes measuring me. He didn't like what he saw.

"So?"

"So you'll do it."

Somebody swore. I saw a man with cards in his hand lay them down. I saw his smile begin to grow, and I saw his eyes wrinkle with humor. All this I saw from the corners of my eyes. I was watching Billings.

He looked at me. Never had I seen a pair of eyes like that. They were careful eyes. Very hard eyes, but careful. This was the most dangerous man I had seen. Yet I doubted if this man would kill. He would see that it was done by someone else. He was too careful to risk it.

That was what I thought then. I was wrong, but it seemed like that.

"Kid, you don't know what you're talking about. John did all right in this town. He could have got rich. You can, too. Together, we can run it."

"I don't need you," I said. "I'm running it now, and I'm running it honest."

He looked at his cigar. He was doing some fast thinking.

"The council wouldn't stand for this," he said. "I know they wouldn't."

"It will be too late for them to object. You're starting now."

His temper exploded then. "Like hell I am! Why you damn fool, I—"

Right then I hit him. My fist cut his words off, and before he could get set, I hit him again. This he had not expected. Gunfighters rarely used their hands, and he was a powerful man who outweighed me by a good fifty pounds.

My second punch knocked him back against the bar, and then I kicked him on the kneecap with a boot heel.

He went down then. He hit right in his dirty sawdust. I reached a hand for him and he grabbed at it with both of his, as I'd expected. And then I hit him on the cheekbone with a short right.

The skin split as if I'd used a knife, and blood started to trickle. Then I stepped back for him to get up. His hand started for his gun but a voice stopped him. "Don't try it, Ben. That's Ryan Tyler."

Something inside him seemed to relax and he sat back down on the floor. It bothered me, because he was a man who could control his emotions. He hated me. He wanted me dead. But he was a careful man.

It was ten to one his games were rigged.

"All right," I said, "you've got a dirty job to do."

Mustang had two guns out and he was looking across them at the room, smiling that tough, reckless smile of his.

"Get used to him, boys. It'll be easier for you. I came up the trail from Texas with him. I seen him kill Leet Bowers. I seen him trim Ollie Burdette down to size and run him out of town. Get used to the idea. He means what he says."

Ben Billings got up slowly and carefully. "Can't we talk this over?"

"No," I said, and motioned him to the door.

"I'll get my coat."

"You won't need it. You'll be warm enough, working the way you will be."

We went, but we weren't alone. Half the place came along to see this. Ben Billings had been boss of the town. He had been the big boss. He had been his own bouncer, often throwing two men out of his saloon at once. He had ordered men killed. He had ordered men beaten. A few he had beaten thoroughly and cruelly with his own hands.

They saw him take the body of John Lang outside. They saw him get water and mop the floor of the marshal's office. And by the time he was through there were three or four hundred people in the street.

This was more than a cleanup job. This was to show the people of Alta that Billings wasn't as big as he had made them believe. It was to show them that a new system had been born. And there were few disapproving looks in the crowd, even from his own followers.

There was an old coat that had belonged to Lang in the office. There were gloves and a hat. "Put these on," I said. "You'll need them digging the grave."

"The ground's frozen!" he protested. "You couldn't dig a grave in a week."

"I hope it doesn't take you that long," I said, "because you'll be mighty tired by that time."

He dug the grave. It was cold and brutal work, with the pick just breaking the ground in tiny flakes. It took him two days and two nights, with time out for meals, and an hour's sleep I allowed him at three intervals. He dug it with Mustang and me spelling each other in two hour tricks.

By the time that grave was dug, the town knew who was marshal. Me, I went back downtown and started checking the gambling joints. We found a controlled wheel in one of Billings' joints, and when Mustang brought in an ax I busted the table right in front of their eyes.

Two more wheels showed evidence of hasty correction. I let them go. "Just keep 'em that way," I said. "You can live on the percentage."

Key Novak was sitting behind his table waiting for us. He looked up at me out of those cold, almost white eyes. Only the look in them was different now. It is one thing when you look at an unknown stranger who is scarcely more than a boy. It is another when you look into those same eyes and know the man is fast with a gun, perhaps faster than you.

Key Novak looked up at me and waited. He hated me, and he was a gunman. He was also a sure-thing operator.

"You got a horse?" I asked him.

"Yes."

"Use him, then, or sell him and take the stage. Your game is closed as of now."

He looked up at me, and I saw his eyelids tighten, the corners of his mouth grow white. He wanted to draw, and he had killed men.

But John Lang had tried it, and John Lang was dead.

"It'll be different with you." I spoke quietly, but there was no mercy in me for the man who had killed a miner and would have shot into him as he lay on the floor. "I'll take your gun away and make you dig your own grave."

He looked at me, his face whiter than I had believed a man's face could be. And then his hands started to shake and there was a glisten of sweat on his brow and upper lip. He got up shakily, and then he walked quickly from the room.

We were keeping our ears open as we worked the town over, but there was no word of Liza anywhere.

Then one night a man lurched up to me on the street. He was acting drunk, but he was cold sober when he spoke. "Heard you asking about a girl named Liza Hetrick. You take a look at that place of Billings' up the canyon."

I grabbed him. "She out there?"

"Word to the wise," he said hoarsely. "You take a look."

109

THIRTEEN

B en Billings' canyon place was six miles out. It was a winding mountain trail, and I took it fast. The gray had been eating his head off and was ready to go, even in that cold. And it was pushing right close to zero.

It was night when I started, the stars so bright they hurt, the night clear and brittle, the snow crunching underfoot and scintillating with a million tiny brilliants. I liked the look of it, liked it fine. Only I wasn't thinking of snow, I was thinking of Liza.

Once I had the gray warmed up a little, I kept him at a fast walk. I didn't want him working up a sweat on a cold night.

Aside from my Smith & Wesson pistols and my rifle, I was carrying a sawed-off shotgun from the marshal's office. It was one of those Colt revolving shotguns that fire four shots. That one I had slung under the buffalo coat that hung to my knees.

One .44 was thrust down into my waistband where I could draw it without pushing the coat back. But I wasn't figuring on it too much.

Leaving the trail when I sighted a light up ahead, I turned off into the trees. When I had walked my horse close, I could see through the top of the window, and there was a woman sitting with her back to me, sitting in a rocker. She was a young woman and the hair was the right color.

111

It looked mighty peaceful, mighty quiet. But when a man has lived as I'd lived, he begins to mistrust the looks of things. He gets cautious, if you know what I mean. And me, I didn't like the look of that frost on the window. There wasn't enough of it.

A body who was a mite suspicious might believe just enough had been scraped away so a man could see in, so he could see just what he was supposed to see.

Getting down from my horse, I walked away through the snow. There was a window on the north side, too. It was frosted to within an inch of the top. So right then I did some fast thinking.

A man going into a tight corner would first investigate the stable, and be mighty careful about it. A man would approach the door only after he was sure the girl was alone.

So I did investigate the stable. There were two horses in it, which meant nothing, because the rig I'd seen outside was a cutter for a two-horse team. There was some harness there, but there was no dampness on the horses, and no snow anywhere in that stable. There were no recent tracks near the stable or the house. But I was getting an idea.

From the window I could see a door, maybe to the kitchen. But I couldn't see anything that was on this side of the entrance. If a man entered and was suspicious, he would watch that kitchen door.

If this was a trap, it was a good one laid by smart men who knew what they were doing, and who knew the sort of man I was. But I hadn't come out all that way just to ride back. Anyway, I always believed in taking the bull by the horns.

So I opened the door and stepped in without knocking, but I didn't just step over the threshold and stop. I ducked low and jumped four feet into the room, then spun a chair around and faced the corner I couldn't see from the outside.

It was covered with a red blanket that reached to the floor.

The girl had got up and backed off, her face strained and pale. And she was no more Liza than I was.

112

"Better close the door, ma'am. Liable to get cold in here."

She hesitated, and put out a hand to steady herself. She was dressed like a ranch woman, but her face was painted, and anybody could tell what she was.

Where I stood, anybody behind that blanket could not see me. If I'd stepped through that door and stopped, I'd have been a sitting duck, but now whoever was there would have to move out from behind that blanket. Nor was I in range from the kitchen door, and as soon as I spoke, I moved.

Walking carefully, the girl crossed and closed the door. The fact that my coming was no surprise, or even the manner of my coming, showed me I had been expected.

"Know anything about a girl named Liza Hetrick?"

"No. . . . No, I never heard of her."

"Who owns this house?"

"Why, I rent it from Mr. Billings."

My eyes never left that curtain and she could see them. She was getting more and more nervous.

By now I'd moved until I had that old sheet-iron stove between me and the curtain. It was a hot stove, and it stood on legs more than a foot high, bringing it more than chest-high on me, and it was wider than me. It was good protection.

The way I stood, only my right side was free of that stove. And that was where my gun hung.

"You behind the curtain," I said. "Come out."

There was no move, no sound.

"You're a crazy fool!" The girl's voice was a little too shrill. "Nobody's back there!"

"All right," I said, "pick up that poker."

She hesitated, then picked it up. "Now lift it shoulder-high and take a full swing with both hands," I said, "and hit that blanket."

"No!" She jerked back, frightened. Then she caught herself. "Why should I do that?"

"Do it!"

113

She touched her lips with her tongue and drew back. "No," she said, "I won't!"

"All right," I said loudly, "I'll shoot into it with a shotgun."

With sudden triumph she cried out, "He hasn't got a shotgun! He's lying!"

She didn't say, "You haven't got a shotgun," as she would have done if she'd been speaking to me, so I knew she spoke for the benefit of whoever was concealed in the house.

And right then that kitchen door slammed open and a man stepped in and said, "Now, Joe!" and he shot.

Only the trouble was, I had my right hand inside my coat. There was a slit inside the pocket of my buffalo coat that enabled me to grasp the gun at my belt or the shotgun, and my coat was unbuttoned.

The shotgun was suspended by a strap inside my coat and that kitchen door grated on a little sand, a scarcely perceptible sound, and I stepped around the stove and shot into the blanket, shot twice, fast as I could pull the trigger. A bullet rang like a bell against the sheet-iron stove, and then I turned and shot past the stove at the man standing in the door to the kitchen.

It was fast, like the wink of an eye. Three shots gone in the fifth part of a second, maybe. And two men dead.

The man in the kitchen door had taken his in the belt. The man behind the blanket had fallen forward, pulling the red blanket down with him. One charge of buckshot had caught him in the face and one in the chest.

There was an acrid smell of gunpowder, and then the sound was gone and the room was empty and I could hear the clock ticking and the sobs of the girl. Something was stinging my arm. Looking down, I was surprised to see blood there.

The girl had drawn back into the corner and was staring at the dead men with horror on her face. I didn't feel sorry for her. She helped set that trap, and she played along with them all the way.

114

One of them was Lang's deputy, the one I'd ordered out of town. The other was a loafer I'd seen around Billings' saloon.

Me, I stood there, looking down at those two men. "Six," I said. "Six and seven."

"What?" She stared at me.

"Nothing," I said, "only you'd better get into town. I don't want you."

"You'll let me go?"

"Sure," I said. "I expect you did what you were told to do."

She seemed dazed. She picked up her coat and a woolen muffler, her eyes avoiding the bodies. I helped her on with her coat. "You'll beat him," she said. "He didn't think you were so smart."

"Hope so," I said.

She wrapped the muffler around her head and tied it under her chin.

"Who is this Liza Hetrick? Are you in love with her?"

"Me? Ma'am, she was a child when I saw her last, but pretty. I guess I was only a kid myself. I . . . I liked her. And her folks were like my own."

"Ben knows something. I know he does. He talks about her as if he does." She paused. "I hope you find her."

"If she's here, where would she be?"

"One of the places in town. Any one of them. Ben owns them all."

She rode back to town with me and I took her to the stage station when the stage was there and put her on it. As she got in, two men started for their horses.

"You," I said. "Get back inside."

"What?"

The shotgun came out from under my coat and they almost tore the door down getting in.

Right there I stayed until that stage was well out of town and making fast time on the hard-packed snow. I walked to the marshal's office then, and Mustang threw down his cigarette as

I came in. "You're a trouble to a man," he said dryly. "I been worried."

So I told him what happened.

"Figured it," he said. "Until a few minutes ago they had four men across the street. My guess is they were to come in fast once they knew you were dead."

He had two shotguns lying on the desk and a sawed-off Henry rifle.

They would have needed more than four men to come in that door with Mustang behind those guns. I'd seen some tough men, but Mustang was born with the bark on. And there was no rabbit in him.

And that night, without further delay, we started a shakedown of the houses in Alta. We started at the first one and worked our way down the street. We embarrassed some folks and frightened others, but house by house we shook the places down. We found nobody held against her will. We found nothing that gave us a lead.

But we gave that town a going over it would never forget, and we started a few people traveling. There was a red-haired man who objected, but Mustang kicked him downstairs and knocked him into the street.

Two weeks passed slowly, but they were weeks of comparative peace. We arrested a couple of men for knife fights, and Mustang caught in action a holdup man who in a misguided moment tried to shoot it out. It was a mistake.

After that, things settled down fast. The town took a second look at the situation and women began to do more shopping than they had done before, and the tough boys sang mighty small. The honest people liked it and the crooks didn't have any choice. Billings came and went about his business and avoided us.

"Too quiet," Mustang said, and I agreed with him.

By the end of February the town had had the most peaceful month in its short history. Murdock came down to see us and told us he was pleased, but even he was wondering how long it would last.

Liza was always on my mind, but I was trying to think it out now. Billings was not a man one could frighten or force into talking. Whatever he might know he did not plan to tell. Yet something had to break.

Meanwhile, we had been checking. The marshal previous to John Lang had been murdered. He had been shot in the back of the head at close range.

John Lang had not then been in town. He had been sent for and promised the job of marshal. We found the letter in the safe, where it had been left through some oversight. The letter was signed "T. J. Farris."

There was nobody in town by that name.

Yet whoever had written that letter had been known to John Lang. John Lang had known him well enough to come all the way from Texas to take the job. Lang had believed him. . . .

Moreover, whoever wrote that letter had been mighty sure he could do what he wanted in town.

Ben Billings was careful. He was never out of our sight. Yet I couldn't forget what that girl had said. Billings knew something about Liza.

We watched him as he went about his business. He did not ride out of town. He was careful, mighty careful. He never stayed anyplace very long.

He was worried, too. He must have known that we knew he was guilty of arranging that plot to kill me, but we had done nothing. And that bothered him.

Business was good. The mines were shipping ore. Everybody seemed happy . . . except me.

Mustang, he was always on the prowl. He would take his horse and ride away, and he would return just in time to take his shift. We had rounded up two more deputies to handle the day shift, which was usually quiet. They were local men, a tough old ex-soldier named Riley and a miner with a bad lung named Schaumberg.

One night I was standing alone on the street and just about to move on when somebody spoke to me from the shadows.

"Don't make a wrong move. Don't try to see who I am. My life wouldn't be worth a plug penny. But look down Lang's back trail."

"Thanks."

"All right." The man in the darkness chuckled. "Worth it to see Billings moppin' the floor!"

Footsteps retreated down a narrow alleyway, and I stood quiet until they were gone. Me, I was pretty sure it had been the gambler with the smile.

We wrote some letters, Mustang and me. We wrote letters to Denver and Cheyenne, because we knew Lang had been both places. We found out he had been in Cimarron and Tascosa. And in Cimarron he had been associated with a gambler known as Ben Blake.

Ben Blake . . . Ben Billings. And the descriptions fitted. The trouble was, that was all. We couldn't tie anybody to them. And nobody in Denver, Cimarron, Tascosa, or Cheyenne knew anything about them, or about anybody known as Farris.

Mustang and me, we sat in the office one night. It was coming on for spring and a soft wind was blowing. I had been around town all day and was getting restless, or maybe it was just the wind.

Mustang, he tipped back in his chair, that long narrow face of his looking uncommon thoughtful. He slid his hat back on his head, showing that cowlick of blond hair.

"You sure was on your own mighty young," he said suddenly. "Wonder you got away from them Indians."

"I had a fast horse. Old Blue."

"Gave him to Liza, didn't you?"

"Well, sort of. She was to ride him."

Mustang rolled him a smoke and when it was lit he said thoughtfully, "You set store by that kid. Maybe she set some by you, too. You're a good-lookin' galoot. All the womenfolks in town say you're handsome. I reckon they could be right. Now, such a girl as that, not seein' many men, she might be so dumb as to fall for you."

"Not much chance."

"S'posin' she did. She have anything to remember you by?"

"Not that I know of."

"Except Old Blue."

"He's prob'ly dead. Old, anyway. And most of the horses were stolen."

Mustang drew deep on his cigarette, and looked superior-like. "Not him," he said. "I seen him today."

FOURTEEN

Come daylight, we rode out there, ready for trouble. Really loaded for bear.

If what Mustang figured was true, Liza would take care of that horse. If she cared a mite about me, she would keep Old Blue close to her.

Mustang, he was a shrewd one. He set around with a poker face most of the time, but he used that head of his, and he reasoned mighty well.

He got to thinking about that girl and that ranch. He reasoned she would keep Old Blue up close to the house. In the stable, prob'ly. He reasoned Old Blue wouldn't get stolen for that reason. Besides, he was mighty old, and no horse thief would want a gelding who was getting along in years.

"Something else," Mustang said. "Whoever this T. J. Farris is, he knows who you are."

"I figure."

"I mean he knows plenty about you. He's gone to some trouble to find out. He even knows things I don't know about you."

"How's that?"

"You'll see. He's been huntin' along your back trail. Maybe to find something to scare you with."

This ranch was a little outfit back in the hills, not far from town, but out of the way. A nice little ranch with pole corrals and rail fences and some good meadowland. There were some stacks of hay put up, and I could see some berries trimmed and up on a fence, like. She was a mighty nice place.

We came riding up mighty slow. Mustang, he had scouted the place, and he had talked to the man who owned it. Or said he owned it. Only now it might be a trap.

Sure enough, Old Blue was there. He still had on his winter coat and looked mighty rough, but it made a lump come in my throat to see him. Why, he must be fourteen years old, maybe older.

Right then, outlaws or no outlaws, trap or none, I wasn't passing up Old Blue. I swung down and went over to the fence.

"Blue," I said. "Good Old Blue!"

His head came up and his ears pricked. He came toward the fence, then stopped, looking at me. "Blue, you old sidewinder! *Blue!*"

Then I reckon I shed some tears. I reckon I did. In front of Roberts and all. With maybe guns trained on me. But this was Old Blue, the horse that had come across the plains with us, the horse my pap rode, the horse that carried me that lonely crying time after Pap was killed. The horse that carried me right up to the ranch where I'd met Liza.

And he knew me. Don't you ever tell me a horse can't remember! He remembered, all right. He came up and I went over that rail fence and put my arms around his neck. And he nuzzled me with his nose.

"Where is she, Blue? Where's Liza?"

And if he could have talked, he would have told me. I believe that. If he could have talked. Only he couldn't. Or . . . could he?

A man was coming down the lane toward us, a tall old man with gray hair, just such a man as Hetrick himself had been. Gave me a start for a minute, only when he came nearer I saw it wasn't him. Nor even much like him.

"Knows you, doesn't he?"

"He should. We went through it together."

"So I was told."

"Told? By Liza? Where is she?"

He drew on his pipe. "No idea. I told him." He gestured at Mustang Roberts. "I'd no idea. Only the horse was left here.

"A man came up one day with the horse. I knew the horse because I'd seen him with the girl. She had brought him with her behind the stage. All she had left, she said, and she was going to keep him.

"This man who was with her, he said to keep the horse. He said to take good care of him. He said one day you'd come along to claim him."

"That I would?"

"What he said. That you would. Named you to me. He said Rye Tyler would be along. That if you wanted him, he was yours. Otherwise I was to give him a home here until he died. With the best of care."

Now, that was funny. That was most odd. What would anybody care about my old horse? Unless . . . maybe he was doing it to please Liza. Right then I felt sort of sick. Maybe he was in love with her, and her with him. Why else would a man care about another man's horse?

But this was getting mixed up. Maybe this gent had no connection with T. J. Farris at all. Maybe he was just somebody who met Liza and fell in love with her. Maybe Liza was happily married now. Maybe she was in a good home and I was wasting my time, and Mustang's too. Why else would a man think so of a horse?

"This man. What did he look like?"

"Quiet-looking man. A cowhand, but no kid. He said his boss wanted the horse left here."

"His *boss?*"

"Uh-huh, that's it."

So it was another blind trail. Who might the boss be? "This cowhand. Where was he from? Who was he?"

Louis L'Amour

"Gave no name. Never saw him before. He gave me a hundred dollars and told me to take care of the horse. I'm a man who likes horses, and he knew it. And any man would like Old Blue."

None of this made sense. In one way, I wasn't so much worried. A man who would think that much of another man's horse wasn't the sort to be mean with a woman. Yet in another way, I was worried. That sort of man might be the kind she could love. And that bothered me. I guess Mustang was right. I was in love with Liza.

And this was another dead end. Or mighty near it.

The thing that had me wondering was why Billings would not talk about his connection with the girl. Especially when he must have known I'd get out of his wool if I took out after Liza.

Yet two months later I was no nearer finding her, and on the day when I again heard of her, I killed my eighth man.

We had occasional trouble with drunken miners, but we usually put them in jail to cool off and sober up. Otherwise it was almighty tame. Then one day a man tried to hold up, of all places, Billings' saloon.

Shouldn't say he tried. He did it. Me, I was back of the office saddling the gray when I heard a shot. I stepped around the horse and was looking along the back doors of the buildings when I saw this door burst open and a man lunge out with a sack in his hand.

He had a gun gripped in the other hand, and I could see a horse waiting. He was headed for that horse when I yelled at him. I told him to hold up there, and be quick.

At that, he might have got away. There was a couple of wagons and a wagon yard betwixt us, and he would have been behind them in two more jumps. But when I yelled he skidded to a stop and came up with his gun.

My bullet nailed him just as he fired. His shot went whining off overhead, seeming closer than it was. Always that way with a bullet when a man is shot at. Always seems close.

When I got to him he was in bad shape. The bullet had hit

124

him in the side and gone through both his lungs and he was breathing blood in bubbles. All the fight was knocked out of him. His gun had fallen where he could have reached it, but he didn't try.

When I leaned over him he spoke mighty bitter. "*You!* That . . . that stopped me! I . . . I had to make my try!"

The holdup man was Ollie Burdette. He looked older, grayer. Yet it had been only a few months since I'd run him out of Mason Crossing.

Yet there was a glint in his eyes, a kind of fading triumph. "I seen her!" I could barely hear the words. "Seen her! You'll never get her now! You'll . . . better man!"

"What?" I grabbed his shoulder. "You saw who?"

He was going fast, and folks were coming, but he was having the last laugh. "I . . . seen Liza!" He spoke with that ugly bubbling sound from bleeding lungs. "Better man than you . . . got her!"

And he died.

Ben Billings scooped up the spilled money. He looked at Burdette, then curiously at me. "You know him?"

How much had Billings heard? What was he thinking?

"Ollie Burdette," I told him, "from over at the Crossing."

Billings looked at the dead man, a curious, thoughtful look on his face. "Strange. . . . A man would think he was fated to die by your gun. You didn't kill him there, so unexpectedly you kill him here." He looked around at me. "Makes a man wonder."

It did, at that.

And was there some other meaning behind the words of Ben Billings? Was he, too, fated to die by my gun?

And that night, back at the office, I thought about it. Who could have guessed such a thing would happen? That from the day Burdette saw me on the street, I was marked by some fate to cut him down? Did he know it in some queer way? Me, I don't set much store by that sort of thing, but it does beat all.

Billings could have killed him, or a dozen men. Yet it was

me. And he was my eighth man, and I had never wanted to kill even one.

Sometimes when I got up in the morning I hated to belt on my gun. Sometimes I just looked at it and wished I could be shut of the whole thing, that I could get clean away from it all, and go someplace where men did not pack guns or shoot to kill.

Maybe you think I could have left my guns off, but I wouldn't have lived an hour. Not one. Too many of that Billings crowd around, or others who wanted my hide.

When Mustang and me took over there had been robberies and murders every night. It was the law of the gun that we brought to Alta, but it was law. Ours was a time of violence, of men fiercely independent, of men who resented every slight and whose only recourse was to the Colt.

It is all very well for those who live in the East to talk of more peaceful means, or for those who live in the later, gentler years, but we were men with the bark on, and we were opening up raw, new country, mustang country, bronco country, uncurried, unbroken, and fierce. Because of the guns I wore, women walked along our streets now, children were going to a small school nearby, and people went to church on Sunday. I wore my guns and the thieves and murderers sat in the shadows and waited for me to fall or to have a moment of carelessness.

I thought of Liza. A better man, he had said. A better man had won her. But better in what sense? What sort of man could be friendly to Billings and be a good man?

One thing I had in that town, I had a friend. No man was ever more understanding or a stronger right hand than Mustang Roberts. He had only three short years of schooling. He read, but slowly. He could write, though not well. But there was in him a purpose and endurance such as I have seen in few men, and a kind of rocklike strength that let me go ahead knowing he would always be at my back, ready to back me up with his guns.

He came in that night after the killing of Burdette and I told him about the last words of the man from Mason Crossing. Then we started talking, as we often did, about the gun fighters who were making names for themselves, about Hickok, Allison, Ben Thompson, and King Fisher.

"You ever run into Ash Milo, the Mogollon gunman?"

"Never did. He wasn't one of the Market Square crowd in Kansas City. That was where I saw Hickok."

Mustang rolled a smoke. "He's a mighty mean man. And pure poison with a gun. I never did see him, either, and never heard tell of him until about two years ago. In those two years he's made a name."

He tipped back in his chair. "He killed six men last year. Hunted down two of them, two big names. Deliberately hunted them. He's mean, he's reckless, doesn't seem to care . . . or didn't at first. This past year he's tapered off a little. Maybe he found something worth living for."

"Don't know much about him. Outlaw, isn't he?"

Seemed to me as I spoke that I'd seen his name on some of the circulars we got in the mail.

"Uh-huh. Stuck up a payroll in Nevada. Then a train, some stages. Killed the marshal at Greener."

"Hope he doesn't come this way," I said. "I want no truck with him. I don't want to kill anybody, not ever."

We talked and loafed through the night and finally when daylight began to show we called the day watch and turned in. After I got into bed I got to thinking about Mustang asking me if I'd known Milo. Maybe the question had been more pointed than I'd believed. . . . No, I was getting too suspicious. Finding double meanings everywhere.

By then I had saved eight thousand dollars. Not so much, maybe, but a sight for a kid with no education who was just twenty-one years old.

Folks in town seemed to like me. And I was getting to know them. The toughs passed me by, glad to be unnoticed, but the

127

businessmen often stopped to talk and their wives would bow to me on the street.

I'd always kept the office looking clean and dusted, but lately I'd taken to dressing up a little myself. I'd discarded the old buckskins, and had taken to wearing tailored black or gray trousers.

Also, I'd started a move to clean up the back yards and junk heaps. Not that I needed any help. All I had to do was drop a word here and there.

But always in the back of my mind was Liza, and I knew I would never feel free until I knew she was all right, and until I was sure she was happy. Sometimes I got to studying about it and trying to put it all together: the fact that Billings knew something about her, that Old Blue had been left at a nearby ranch, that Ollie Burdette had known something.

We had tried to find out where Ollie Burdette had been hiding out before he came to Alta, but we got nowhere. His trail vanished utterly. For two months there was a complete blank space in his life.

Mustang never stopped digging around. Sometimes he would come up with odd comments that started me thinking. Mustang was a patient man, and when I said he would make a good Pinkerton, I was right. If I was a crook I'd not want him on my trail.

One day he came into the office just after I got up. It was right after lunchtime. We had stood the night watch, as usual.

"This here Ash Milo," he said; "he killed another man. Killed an outlaw named Ruskin."

"Heard of Ruskin."

"Uh-huh. Bad man. Woman trouble. Ruskin never could leave them alone."

"Where'd this happen?" I was just making conversation. I didn't care where it happened. Or anything about either of them.

"Thieves' hideout. Place back on the plateau called Robbers' Roost."

Of course, I knew about the place. There was an area out there several hundred miles square that was a known hideout for thieves and killers. We had no big crime in Alta, so it didn't affect us, but every time a bank, train, or payroll was taken, the bandits took off for the Roost. And no posse dared to go after them. Only one ever tried. The two men who survived had been shot to doll rags.

"This Ash Milo is the boss back in there."

"Yeah?"

"You never knew him?"

"Not me."

Mustang, he let his chair legs down to the floor. "That's funny, Rye, because he knows you."

FIFTEEN

That took a few minutes to make itself felt. Then I said, "By reputation, you mean."

"No. He knows you."

I scowled, thinking back. There was no Ash Milo anywhere in my memory. Of course, a man meets a lot of folks, time to time, and back on the cattle drive there had been a lot whose names I never knew. The same was true of Wichita, Dodge, Uvalde, and Kansas City.

There had been a lot of gun-packing men at Red River Crossing, too. But no Ash Milo that I could remember.

"What gives you that idea?" I said at last.

"Because the word's out. None of that gang are to start any trouble over here. They stay out of town and they pull nothing crooked in this town. He told them flatly you were bad medicine and to be left alone."

"Good for him. Saves trouble."

Mustang Roberts wasn't happy about it, I could see. Something was biting him, eating at him. He got up and paced the floor and he was studying this thing out. He had a good head and he thought of a lot of things.

"This may be it, Rye. This may be it."

"What?"

"The tie-up. The link between Billings, Liza and Old Blue."

131

LOUIS L'AMOUR

"No connection that I can see."

"Me, neither. But it's got the feel. I think it's there."

That night I made my rounds about eleven o'clock. That was the best time, because by then the boys would be liquored up enough to think they were mighty big, but knowing my gun was around usually kept them mighty sober. Most times all I had to do was walk around and show myself.

While I was walking, I got to thinking. It might be. Maybe there was something to this idea. It might just be the connection between Liza, Billings, and the fact that Ollie Burdette had seen Liza recently.

Pausing against the side of a building, I thought that over. Ollie Burdette had dropped from sight for several months, and during that period he must have seen Liza. On Robbers' Roost he would be out of sight and so would she. And nobody would do much talking about it.

And Burdette had said a better man had Liza. Had he meant Ash Milo?

Of course, I knew a little about Milo. And since Mustang had mentioned him I'd begun remembering things and hearing more. I expect I'd been hearing them before without paying them no mind.

Many considered him the most dangerous gunman west of the Rockies. And they weren't giving him second place to Hickok, Earp, or any of them.

Returning to the office, I went through the files. The holdup in Nevada seemed to have been the beginning of his Western career.

It had been a job with timing and finish. It had been planned carefully and had come off without a hitch, and must have taken place while I was on that cattle drive.

The killing of the marshal revealed another side to his character. The account in the files told of Milo's literally shooting the marshal to rags. It had been the act of a killer, of a man in the possession of terrible fury or a homicidal mania . . . or of

132

an extremely cold-blooded man who wanted to shock people into absolute fear.

The marshal before John Lang had kept careful files, and reading what I could find on Milo gave me a picture of a sharp, intelligent, thoroughly dangerous man who shot as quick as a striking snake and asked no questions.

The picture was not pretty. At least twice he had killed men because they got in the way at the wrong time. And when they were only too anxious to get out of his way. He was a man utterly ruthless, but also a man who seemed driven by some inner fury.

Ash Milo shaped up like no easy proposition. He was a very dangerous man, but he did not fit the description of any man I knew. So that part could be ruled out.

Nevertheless, the thought that he might have Liza worried me. And where else could she be? Thinking of Liza made me think of Old Blue. When I awakened the next day at noon, after working the night hitch, I saddled up and rode out to see him.

He trotted to the fence to greet me. It was good to see the old fellow. I fed him some sugar, slapped him on the shoulder, ran my fingers up through his mane . . . and stopped.

My fingers had found something. Something tied or tangled there. Slowly, knowing it was by the feel, I parted the long hairs of the mane and looked at a folded square of paper. Untangling the mane, I untied the knots that held it in place.

It opened out, and I knew the handwriting.

Liza!

My heart pounding, I held it a moment before beginning to read. Then, finally, I lowered my eyes.

Dearest Rye:
    Please don't try to find me. Go away. To find me will only bring you heartbreak and misery, and possibly death. I am all right, and I am happy to know you are well, and away from here. Go! If you love me, please go!
                                                            LIZA

So . . . at last a message. The gap bridged by a few simple words. But she was sending me away.

That I did not think of at first. Only that she had to be close. She was near.

Vaulting the fence, I stepped into the leather and went to the ranch house at a dead run.

The old man had been washing dishes and he came to the door drying his hands on a towel. "Figured to see you," he said. "That girl was here."

"When was it?"

"Two days ago, along about sundown. She come with that puncher and two others. Looked mighty mean, they did. She went down to see the horse and two of them stayed close all the time. She asked if you had been around and seemed pleased when I told her you was some happy about the horse."

"How's she look?"

"Mighty pretty. Beautiful, even. Hair's pretty, and a good figger. Looks well fed, but ain't fat. Just nice-like. But . . . well, kind of worried. Upset, maybe."

"Where'd they go?"

"Like I said, it was sundown when they showed. By the time they left, it was clean dark. I couldn't even see to the gate, but I figure they went south."

No matter how many questions I asked, that was all he could tell me, except that they had not let her out of their sight, and the one puncher he had seen before had this time stayed well away from the house.

"Mighty interested in you," he added. "Asked a sight of questions." He returned to washing dishes. "Seemed to me they picked that time to get here so's they could leave in the dark. I figure it was planned."

Descriptions of the men meant nothing to me, nor could he tell me if any one of the three seemed to have authority. Liza had been treated politely and with respect, but they had never left her alone with him for a minute.

Mustang was sitting on the walk with his back against the

134

wall of the building when I returned to the office. I told him what had happened and showed him the note. He frowned over it, reading poorly as he did, but then he looked up and said, "Man asking for you. He's at the hotel." Mustang got up. "It's that gent from Denver. That Denison what's-his-name."

"All right. I'll go see him. He say what he wanted?"

"No. Only he asked a lot of questions about you. Asked about Burdette, and about the fight at Billings' place."

The hotel was a long two-story building of unpainted lumber, some weathered by wind and rain. It had been put together in a hurry to accommodate the sudden influx of visitors while the town was booming.

Denison Mead sat by the fire alone when I walked into the lobby. The place was almost empty, usual for that time of day.

The room was big and there was a homemade settee, some huge old leather chairs, and the desk at one end of the room with the stairway to the rooms opposite it. The floor was bare and there were only a few crude paintings on the wall, and one good drawing of a bucking horse, traded to the proprietor for a meal two years before.

Mead got up to shake my hand, and seemed really pleased to see me. His eyes searched my face curiously, and then he waved at a chair and sat down himself.

"Tyler, I'll get right to business. When I first met you in Denver I was struck by your resemblance to somebody I knew. When you answered my questions, your answers told me without doubt you were the person whom I thought you to be."

"I'm afraid I don't quite get you, mister."

"I told you I was a lawyer handling mining property. My firm also handles the Blair estate. In fact, they are one of our oldest clients."

This Mead seemed like a nice fellow, but whatever he had in mind, I didn't know. And he was taking a long time getting to it.

"Tyler, do you have anything that belonged to your mother?"

"A picture, that's all. Everything Pap kept was lost in that Indian raid."

"A picture? Do you have it?"

When I settled in town I began carrying the picture in my pocket instead of keeping it in the saddlebags, so I had it with me. I took it out and handed it to him and he smiled. "Of course! Virginia Blair! I'd know the face anywhere, although I've only seen pictures of her myself."

"Blair?"

"Her maiden name. The family was fairly well off, Tyler. Not wealthy, but substantially fixed. And with a good position socially."

That meant nothing to me until he told me I'd been left some money. Rather, Ma had been left it. Some money and a good-sized farm in Maryland and Virginia. It was more than a thousand acres.

"There's a nice home on it, some stables. They used to raise horses in the old days." He sat back and lit a cigar. "It's all yours, of course. The family was upset when she married your father, but they were sorry for their attitude later, when it was too late. We tried to locate your mother, but had no luck.

"Now, if you'll take my advice, you'll give up all this and come East. You seem to know stock. You've had experience breaking horses. You could probably do very well back there."

Nothing like this had ever come into my mind. I'd have to study it well, yet all the time I was explaining this to him, I was thinking that back East I wouldn't have to carry a gun. And there was small chance anybody would have heard of Ryan Tyler, the gun fighter.

It would be a good thing . . . and then I remembered Liza.

Her note had told me to go away, but I read more into it than that. She was afraid of what would happen to me if I stayed, and if I persisted in trying to find her. But me, I had my own ideas.

So I got up. "Mr. Mead, I'm taking your advice. I'll go back

East and make my home there. You go ahead and get it all fixed up so I can take over. But first I've got a job to do."

He got up, too. "Tyler," he warned, "be careful. I know something of the situation here. I've been kept informed. You've made this town peaceful, but only on the surface. There are men here who hate you and fear you. Make one slip and they'll be on you like a pack of wolves."

"Yes, sir. You get those papers fixed up. I'll be back."

So I walked out on the street, knowing as I walked that my decision was right. This was what I should do. It was a good time to go . . . and, after all, why should I look for Liza? She was with somebody else. If she hadn't made her choice, at least she was doing all right. And I had no actual reason to believe she was living as she was through any reason but her own. So that was over. I'd go back East and stay.

Mustang was pacing the floor when I came in. He turned sharply around. "Got news for you! I went out and hunted up the tracks of those folks who visited Old Blue. They headed south, right into the rough country, and they took a trail that only goes one way."

"Where?" I asked the question, knowing the answer.

"They went to the Roost. And one of those riders was a woman."

Liza . . . and Ash Milo.

Everything had been pointing that way and I couldn't see it until now. Sure enough, that had to be where Ollie Burdette had holed up after leaving the Crossing, and where he'd seen Liza with "a better man." It tied everything into one neat package, and it was the explanation for Billings' knowledge, and why he would not talk. It was common gossip around town that Billings had connections at the Roost.

It explained everything . . . or almost everything.

People all over this part of the country had a justified fear of the Roost and its riders. No rancher would talk. Some were friendly to the outlaws, but even honest ranchers refused to risk incurring their anger. Robber's Roost lay somewhere on a plateau among a network of canyons, a country unknown to any but themselves.

How many outlaws were in there? Some said fifty, but most said it was nearer a thousand. It was the main hideout on the Outlaw's Trail, which stretched from Canada to Mexico through the Rocky Mountain region. And at the Roost, and for miles around, Ash Milo was king.

Unless a man knew the trails, he had no chance of finding his way in. Or so they said. That was the story, all right.

The names of the leaders of the Roost gang were notorious. Ash Milo was the boss, but there were others, names feared all through the West; Sandoval, Bronco Leslie, Chance Vader, and Smoky Hill Stevens. All of them wanted in a half-dozen states, all men who were handy with guns.

And that was where Liza was, among a lot of outlaws. But she didn't want me to come. All right, I wouldn't.

"This Milo," Mustang Roberts said, "he knows you, all right. He knows a lot about you."

"Stories get around."

"Sure. And I thought I'd heard them all, but the grapevine from the Roost has one story I never heard."

"What's that?"

Mustang Roberts took his time. He pushed his hat back on his head and put a boot up on the desk. His spur jingled a mite. He began to build him a smoke.

"One thing I never heard," he said, touching his tongue to the paper. "That you killed a man named McGarry."

SIXTEEN

Mustang Roberts started me thinking again. He got me to wondering, and an hour before daylight I had my mind made up.

Mustang had turned in, as the night was quiet and he was tired from the riding he'd done that day. Me, I put a saddle on the gray, shoved the new Winchester .73 I'd bought into the boot, and then I belted on one gun and shoved the other into my waistband.

First thing, I switched my shirt and left my badge on the table. Where I was going a badge was an invitation to get shot. The shirt I put on had no pin holes left by the badge. Nor did I shave. Right then I was growing a mustache, which was well along, and I trimmed it a little, but let the stubble of beard stay. Then I shrugged into a coat and packed a bait of grub out to the gray.

We took the trail just as the sky was lightening. Nobody needed to tell me what I was riding into. There was no way this trail could miss leading into trouble. Maybe Liza wanted to live with outlaws. Maybe she was Ash Milo's girl, and maybe she wasn't. But I was going to know.

Leaving town by the trail, I turned off up a dry canyon. It was a long ride I had before me, so I let the gray make his own speed. In later years they said the Roost was farther south, but the time I rode into that country the outfit was located in a canyon back of Desolation, not far off the Green River.

It was very hot. Back in the canyons there was no breeze. Soon my gray shirt turned dark with sweat and my eyes had to squint to stand the glare.

There was no sound but the sound of my horse's hoofs and the creak of the saddle. Once in a while a stone rolled underfoot. So it was I started into that rough, wild country, unexplored except by Indians and outlaws, and most of it unknown even to them.

The way I figured, it would be midafternoon before Mustang Roberts realized I was gone. Then he would figure out where I'd headed. Shrewd as he was, he'd guess right the first time. But I'd be long gone then and he'd resign himself to sitting out my stay.

Several times I saw antelope, and once I frightened a mountain lion away from a big-horn sheep.

This was far-off country, wild and lonesome country. It was big country, and I'd seen city men shrink from the immensity of it. Some men are built for this kind of country, and some aren't. I guess my Maker shaped me for the land that we had to shape. I liked it.

There was small chance any of these outlaws would know me as the marshal of Alta. They had been denied the town by Ash Milo, and if I was lucky I'd get well back into that country, looking like an outlaw on the drift.

The gray liked it. He was always a good trail horse, happier when he was going. He was a saddle bum like me, liking the dust of far trails, the smell of pines and sweat, and he would prick his ears at every hill we came over, at every turn we rounded.

Most of the time I rode off to one side of the dim trail. I rode alongside the pines, or took the far side of a ridge, or kept under cover. It was smart in two ways: It would keep me from being seen as long as possible, and if I was seen I'd look like a man on the dodge.

Twice I made short camps and slept a little, then I pushed on. Time enough to take it easy when I began to get close. Then I would have to look careful.

Nobody in Alta knew where the Roost was. Maybe Ben Billings, but he never went there. He was never out of sight long enough. Oh, probably some of the men who came and went around town did know, but nobody who would talk to me or who would have helped me. So I'd never tried to find out, and now I was glad.

I wouldn't want anybody remembering that the marshal of Alta had been inquiring about trails.

Once into the rougher country, I took my time. Skirting Indian Head peak, I crossed the end of the Roan Cliffs and rode into Nine Mile Valley. It was long and empty, unmarked by trails, and pointed southeast, the way I wanted to go. There were cliff dwellings along the canyon walls, and rocks covered with Indian writing. Several times I saw arrowheads and broken pottery.

With a three-day growth of beard on my face and my clothes dusty from travel, I was beginning to look the part. Also, I was getting wary.

Everywhere was rock. Rocky cliffs and crags, great mesas rising abruptly, shelves of rock and plateaus of rock. It was pink and white, with long streaks of rust red or maroon, all carved by wind and rain into weird shapes and giant forms. Huge pinnacles pointed their ghostly fingers at the sky. It was a land shaped like flames, a land riven and torn, upset and turned over and upset again.

I rode down long corridor canyons to the echoing of my horse's hoofs against the sounding boards of the great walls, walls that sometimes pressed close together, and at other times spread wide.

Suddenly the canyon bent northeast, and I followed it. Here was a creek, and I watered the gray, then loosened the girth.

It was late afternoon. It was very hot and I was very tired. In all this vast desert through which I was riding there seemed to be nothing and no one. Lying down on the grass beneath some willows, I stretched out with my hat over my eyes.

Awakening suddenly, I saw that the gray's head was up and that his ears were pricked. With one quick move I was on my feet. When I see a horse like that, even swelling himself a little as he gets set, I know he's going to whinny. My left hand grabbed his nostrils and my right his neck just as he started, and I stopped him. He shied a little, frightened at my sudden move, then stood still.

Listening, I could hear voices. They were some distance off, but seemed to be coming nearer.

My position was behind the willows and out of sight, if nothing attracted their attention. Gray knew he was supposed to keep quiet now, so I released him and dropped my hand to my holstered gun. It was in place. So was the one behind my belt.

Then I picked up my hat and moved back beside my horse, listening and ready.

At first I heard nothing. Whoever it was had stopped talking. Then I heard their horses' hoofs, and, peering through the willows, I saw them.

Neither was a man I had seen before. One wore a black vest over a dark-red shirt. He was a lean, dark man. The other was sandy-haired and freckled, and from his saddle he could have been a Texan. They drifted on by and were almost past me when I heard the redhead call the other one "Bronc." This could be Leslie, the Malheur County badman.

Stepping into the leather, I slow-walked my horse to a point where I could watch them. The afternoon was almost gone, but here was a chance to find my way right to the hideout at the Roost.

If I tried getting closer alone, I might manage it, but if I rode in with Bronco Leslie, I'd be asked few questions. Pushing the gray, I moved out into the open until I could see them plainly.

About the same time they heard me and drew up, waiting.

Bronco Leslie had a scar over one eye and his eyes were the blackest I'd ever seen. His face was thin and drawn down, and he had a quick, nervous way about him. That I saw right off.

"Where you goin'?" he asked, mighty rough.

Drawing up the gray with my left hand, I said, "Hunting the Roost. I figured you boys might be heading that way."

"What made y' figure that?" Red demanded.

This was touch and go, and I knew it. Any moment a wrong word could start somebody shooting, but in some ways it was less risky with men like this. They were good men with guns, and a man who knows guns doesn't fool around. He knows they can kill.

I grinned at them. "Where else would a man go in this God-forsaken country?"

Red looked thoughtful. I saw his eyes taking in the build of my horse, obviously no cow pony, and the rig of my saddle.

"Do I know you?" Bronc asked.

"Damned if I know," I said frankly. "But this ain't my country. Had me some trouble over to Leadville and decided to head west."

This was safe enough, because just a few days before three men had broken jail in Leadville. The three had never been identified, and little was known of them. It had been rumored they were members of the James gang.

"Far's that goes," I said, "I don't know you."

Leslie stared at me. I could see he had no liking for me and was suspicious. I could guess he was figuring what would happen if he'd open the ball with a gun.

But Bronc Leslie was a careful man. He looked me over a little and decided matters could wait. Anyway, if I had a chance out here, I would have none at the Roost.

Red made the peace move. "I'm Red Irons," he said. "This here is Bronco Leslie."

"I'm Choc Ryan," I said, "from down in the Nation."

We drifted along, not saying much. Leslie took to dropping

back a little, and as I liked nobody behind me, I'd drop back
with him. He didn't like it much, but he didn't make an issue
of it, either.

"I'm mighty hungry," I said. "Will we make it tonight?"

"Late," Red told me.

Can you imagine country like that country was then? And
not much changed, even now. A lost land, a land quiet under
the sun, where only the wolves prowled and where the buz-
zards swung on lazy, easy wings. A land unpeopled and still,
where the sun slowly sank, and from the cliffs the shadows
reached out, filling the canyons to the brim with darkness.

Ghostly footfalls echoed against the walls, saddles creaked,
and Red lifted a lonesome voice in song, singing "Zebra Dun,"
and then "Spanish Is a Lovin' Tongue."

It was mighty pleasant riding, mighty pleasant. Only, up
there ahead of me waited a bunch of men who, if they guessed
who I was, would kill me quick. Up ahead waited death, and I
rode alone into a lonely land from which no officer of the law
had ever returned alive, and where Ash Milo, the man I
sought, was king.

Every footfall might be taking me closer and closer to my
death. Yet each took me closer to Liza, and closer to the
solution of my problem. And after this, if I lived, I would be
free.

It was sundown before we made a turn, and by then the cliffs
had turned red and gold with the setting sun. Tall spires like
church steeples loomed ahead. The cliffs, in those last minutes
before darkness filled the canyon, closed in and grew higher,
until we were like ants walking between those gigantic walls.

In the bottom of the canyon it got dark mighty quick. "Many
in there?" I asked.

Red struck a match and lit a smoke. "Couple dozen at
headquarters."

"Know a gent named Ruskin?"

Bronc looked around at me. This was a feeler I was putting

out, wanting to get a line on Ash Milo without bringing up his
name. Ruskin was safe, because if rumors were right he was
the man Milo had trouble with. Also, according to the hand-
bills, Ruskin was from the Nation.

"Friend o' yours?"

"Not him. . . . Well, we had trouble. Come near a shoot-
out. I was just figurin' I'd best watch myself if he was around."

"He was," Red said. "But he ain't."

Leslie spoke up, real satisfied-like. "He's dead. He made a
play for a girl Ash Milo likes, an' Milo up and killed him."

"Ruskin was s'posed to be bad."

"Hell!" Leslie spat. "None of them are bad compared to the
boss. I never seen a man in the world could sling a gun with
him!"

From another gunman, this was high praise, and me, I
figured I'd best start looking at my hole card. Only it might
already be too late. If this Milo was as good as they said, I
might not stand a chance. But I didn't believe that. Not many
gun fighters will believe they don't stand a chance.

For the next hour of riding I heard a lot about Ash Milo.
Bronc Leslie, who had few enthusiasms, had one. It was Milo.

"He's too touchy for my taste," Red said. "A man has to walk
on his toes around him. I never seen a man grab iron so quick,
over nothin'."

This Leslie did not deny. "He's touchy, all right," he admitted. "And maybe he shoots too quick. Someday he'll kill the
wrong man."

I'd heard that before. That was what Logan Pollard advised
me against. He used to talk to me of that, even while telling
me I was good. "You're fast, kid," he'd say, "one of the fastest I
ever saw, but watch it. You'll shoot too quick and get the
wrong man someday.

"Gunmen," he said, "get worse as they get older. They get
to figuring everybody is after them. A man has to quit before
he gets to that point. That's why I quit. That's why I'm lucky to
have Mary."

145

Neither of them said anything more about Ash Milo's girl, and I didn't want to ask questions. Only, if I was to find out, now was the time. Turning into the narrow canyon back of a plateau, I took a chance and commented, "Hell of a place for a woman! How'd he ever get one to come back here?"

"Him?" Red chuckled. "He's a mighty handsome man, and he's got a slick tongue with the ladies. She come willin', I guess, only he watches her mighty close, so I reckon she'd leave if she had her chance."

Leslie spat. "Too slim for my taste," he said. "I never could figure that in Ash. Nothin' between 'em either. He's tryin' to win her honest. Don't know why he fools around like that."

Red was just a black figure in darkness. "She's all right," he said quietly. "A mighty fine girl. She sure fixed me up that time after I got shot. Mighty gentle an' mighty sweet."

The high black wall of the canyon was split by a towering cleft, a narrow opening down which the wind gushed like a strong flow of water. When I looked ahead, all was darkness, with only the narrow strip of gray sky above us. This crack was mighty narrow, and, as I was to discover, mighty long.

When we had been riding maybe a hundred steps, Leslie drew up.

"Three safe men," he said aloud.

"Who?" The voice sounded as if from a cavern.

"This here's Leslie, Jim. Red's with me, an' a new man, name of Choc Ryan."

"Ride ahead, then." After a minute the voice added, "If that new man ain't all right, he'll never ride back out of here."

Me, I had a kind of queasy feeling in my stomach about that time. Riding down that narrow crack to get out of here was going to be rugged, mighty rugged.

"Right back there," Leslie said, "one o' the boys got hisself killed. A man don't speak at the right time, the guard start shootin'. This feller was drunk. It was a bad time to be drinkin'."

For maybe a quarter of a mile it was like that, and then we

146

dipped down into a canyon and ahead of us on a sort of flat we could see lights in some cabins.

"There's the Roost, Choc," Red said. "She ain't much, but she's home, and she's safe. No marshal or sheriff ever seen it."

SEVENTEEN

Right then I was tired, and I'd no right to be, because I was going to have to be on my toes. Just when I would see Ash Milo I had no idea, but I was hoping it would not be tonight.

Worst of all, I kept racking my brain over what Mustang Roberts had told me: that I was known to Ash Milo. I couldn't remember him or anybody he might be. But if he knew me, I wouldn't be Choc Ryan much longer. I'd be Rye Tyler, and dead.

With the weariness of the long ride behind me, all my spirits drained into my boots. How was I to see Liza? Suppose she wasn't even here? If I did see her, what could I accomplish? What fool's errand was this, anyway? I was crazy. . . .

Only I was here.

We got down at the stables and put our horses in stalls. There were some of the finest horses in that barn that I ever did see, and I know horses. They were horses built for speed and bottom. Nobody was going to run these boys down on ordinary horses. Yet I wasn't worried about the gray. He was one of the runningest horses I ever did see. And he could walk the legs off a coon hound.

Leslie took off and we followed him. There was a long building with lighted windows, and we went to that. A boarding-house, sort of.

149

Inside, two, three men sat around drinking coffee. One was just eating. He looked tired and some beat, and he had a bloody bandage on his arm. He looked up as we came in. They all looked at me, but nobody spoke.

Leslie, he done the honors. "Choc Ryan," he said, "from the Nation."

None of them said anything, and then a big Negro came out of the kitchen with a platter of meat and potatoes and put it down beside the tin plate and eating tools. That big black boy's picture was on a poster in my office in Alta. He was wanted for murder. He'd strangled a guard and broke jail.

There was a pot of coffee on the table and I filled cups for Leslie, Red, and myself.

The man with the wounded arm glanced at me. "What d'you know? A gent!"

I grinned at him. "Ain't that," I said, "on'y these fellers are tougher than me. I figure I better butter 'em up a little."

He chuckled and we all settled down to eat. But my comment seemed to set right, and they sort of settled down.

There was a big man across the table with his shirt open almost to his navel. He had a hairy chest and hair climbed up his neck.

"I'm from the Nation," he said.

Here it comes, I thought. Now they ask me questions. Only he just said, "Where'd you live?"

"On the Cimarron," I said. The trail drive had come through that country and I knew that Leet Bowers had him a hangout on the Cimarron. This fellow might know of that.

He made a few comments on that Oklahoma country, and I added a few of my own, enough for him to know I'd been there, all right.

We turned in, bunking on the grass under the trees near the long bunkhouse. None of us wanted to sleep inside, and especially me. By this time I was feeling trapped enough, and I was worried a great deal. This was a tighter fix than I'd reckoned on, and I could see they didn't trust me none at all.

150

Not that anything about me failed to ring true. I knew I measured up. But men on the dodge can't afford to be anything but cautious, and I was a stranger.

The next day we puttered around. I curried my horse and found some corn for him. They had plenty of corn, growing their own, and the men took turns hoeing it. Corn-fed horses will outrun any hay-fed horse, and lazy as some of these men might be, they knew they had to have fast horses with plenty of strength.

Second day I picked up a hoe and walked out there. Nobody said nothing, but when I returned after a couple of hours, I saw it set well with them.

Besides it gave me a chance to look around without being too obvious about it. Any man who uses a hoe leans on it some, and while leaning, I looked the place over.

There were maybe ten buildings. Three or four were houses. Behind one of them I could see a woman's clothes on a line. Unless there was more than one woman, that was where Liza would be. It gave me a lift just to be that close.

But right next door there was another house and two men sat on the stoop. I noticed that at least one of them was there all the time. Nobody was going to get close to her without trouble, that was sure.

There wasn't much talk around, and none about her. I did hear a man say the boss was mighty touchy, and he didn't sound very happy about it.

One thing I could see, plain enough: Whatever else Ash Milo might be, he had this tough bunch buffaloed to a fare-thee-well. Nobody wanted any part of him, and that included Leslie and Sandoval.

There was one man there who was a little on the pushy side. It was Chance Vader.

Second day there, I saw him. He was slick. Smooth-shaved and wearing sideburns, he had pressed pants all the time, and he kept his boots shined up. He wore two guns and he wore

151

them low. Me, I am a looking-around man. I saw he had another gun inside his shirt. That was something to remember.

Chance Vader duded up a good bit and he played cards a lot, and watching him, I saw his eyes straying toward that little gray stone house where Liza was. He looked toward it a lot, and sometimes he strayed toward it, but not often.

Once one of the men in front of the house next door got up and walked over to him. This was a big, burly man called Smoky Hill.

I heard raised voices and finally Chance turned and walked back. Red was sitting with me, and he said, low-voiced, "Trouble there. Chance is too proud of hisself."

Talk around was that Chance had killed six men, four of them sure-enough bad men.

He was salty, that was for true. Anybody tangling with him would have to go all the way.

There was a saloon, but I stayed away from it. I hung around the stables, took care of my horse, cleaned my guns, and listened to talk. Sometimes we pitched horseshoes.

All this time I saw nothing of Ash Milo. But I learned that he didn't come around very much. He stayed up on the hill in a house he had. "Reads a lot," Red said. "Always after papers and magazines. But he knows what's going on, for all of that."

It was Red told me that Milo scattered crumpled newspapers all over the floor before he got into bed. He wasn't taking any chances on somebody sneaking up on him in the dark.

No way I could see for me to get close to Liza. Not even to let her know I was there. And that had to be done.

Oddly enough, it was Chance Vader who brought it about. Right off, he didn't like me much. He would be looking at me with a cynical smile, and even Leslie noticed it. Leslie didn't like me, either. He didn't trust me. Maybe he didn't trust anybody. But he liked me better than Chance.

One day he said to me, "You watch that slick-ear. He'll start on the prod. He's mean. He likes to kill, and he's building a reputation."

"Thanks," I said.

One day I was hoeing corn and had just put down the hoe when I heard a call. "Hey, Choc!"

It was Smoky Hill, and he was standing in front of what I called the guardhouse.

Brushing off my hands, I walked up there. My mouth was dry and my stomach felt funny, and here I was, right close to Liza. If it was sure enough her.

"Look," Smoky Hill said, "I got to leave here for a little while an' that damn Vader's around. You take my place, will you?"

"If Vader comes up here, what do I do?"

He looked at me real cold. "Nobody talks to that girl but Milo. You hear that? That means you. But I know you're all right. You don't drink, an' you're steady. You mind your own affairs. I been watchin' you." He hitched his gun belt. "If that Vader comes up here, you stop him. If he gives you an argument, I'll be hearing about it, and I'll be along."

So he walked off down the hill and I sat down on the step, my heart pounding.

Liza was in that house next door, and we were in full sight of the camp, and I had to get word to her I was here. But *how*?

And then all of a sudden it was easy. Out of the corner of my eye I saw her standing at the window, just behind the curtain. So I took off my hat and put it down on the stoop. I hoped she'd know me.

Stooping forward to pick up a stone, I glanced at the window. She was standing there with the curtain drawn back, slim and straight and lovely, not fifteen feet away, and she knew me. I could see it by the white set of her face. Then she gestured. She meant for me to go.

Picking up the stone and a few others, I started casually tossing them at a can, like a man killing time. When I stooped for more stones I shook my head and showed her two fingers, meaning that the two of us would go. She gestured at me again.

153

And then I heard feet walking.

Chance Vader was standing there sneering at me. "So? You got your eye on the girl, too? She seems ready enough to play."

This was real trouble, and I got up. Worse, there was an odd, puzzled look in Vader's eye.

"Mighty funny," he said, staring at me. "She never looks at me, but you she signals to. Now I wonder. . . ."

"You do your wondering down the hill," I said. "My orders are to keep men away."

He looked at me and I could see in his eyes that he wanted to kill me, but that wasn't as much on his mind right now as something else.

"You got me puzzled," he said. "I seen you before." He turned his head a mite, the way some folks do, studying me. "And it wasn't in the Nation. I never been in the Nation."

"You go back down the hill," I said.

Surprisingly enough, he turned and started to walk off. Then he turned around. "Got it!" he said. His voice was hoarse with surprise. "Denver! You're Ryan Tyler!"

Smoky Hill was coming. He was almost loping. He was still some distance off.

"Rye Tyler," Vader said, "from Alta!"

There was no choice now. Not if we were to get out of here alive. I had wanted never to kill another man, even one several times a killer, such as this one. Yet if this man told his story, I was a dead man, and worse, Liza would never have her chance. I knew now she was not here willingly.

Chance Vader's eyes were shining. There was a cruel triumph in the man. I saw his eyes suddenly sharpen, and his hand moved. Whether he intended to shoot, I'll never know. My hand dropped to my gun and he was a split second slower.

My gun cleared leather and exploded. The bullet hit him right over the belt buckle just as his gun muzzle started to tip upward. Stepping one step to the side to cause him to shift aim, I fired again, spotting this one carefully over his shirt pocket. It should have killed him, but it didn't.

His lips were parted in a wide grin and he had even white teeth, mighty nice teeth. A bullet whipped past my skull and then my left-hand gun bucked. It was the first time I'd ever used two guns, and I was surprised when the bullet broke his elbow. But Smoky Hill was running up the slope, and there was no time to be lost. I stepped in closer, both guns hammering.

For the first time I desperately wanted to kill a man. I had to kill him. Liza's future was at stake, and my life. When I stopped shooting I was standing over him.

Smoky Hill caught my arm as I was reloading. "Take it easy, Choc! He's finished!"

"Rye!" Vader got it out, his eyes glittering in triumph at me, straining with effort. How he managed it I'll never know. How a man shot up like that could even draw a breath I don't know. But he said it again. *"Rye!"*

"Hell!" Somebody spoke wonderingly. "Dyin', an' he wants a drink!"

Standing back, thumbing shells into my guns, I knew it wasn't a drink he wanted, and I was hoping he couldn't say the other name. If he said it I would die here, only with my guns loaded I wouldn't go out by myself. I'd take a few along for company.

Chance Vader had been fast, all right. He had been fast and dangerous and he had sand. Lying there on his back with his lifeblood staining the gravel under him, he still wanted me dead.

But then it was too late. His eyes glazed over and I stepped back, slipping one gun into my waistband.

They stood around, a dozen of them, staring at me. I had no idea what to expect, but I had my gun in my hand. It might make the difference.

"You saved me a job," Smoky Hill said. "You sure did."

Somebody said, looking at the nine bullets I'd put into Vader, "Figured Vader was fast, but—"

"He was fast," Smoky Hill said grimly. "I know he was fast. Only Choc here was faster." He pointed at the body. "And shot straighter. Look. One over the belt buckle, one through the face, and not one of the others missed the heart by over three inches!"

They all looked at me again, sizing me up, getting it straight in their minds. I had outshot Chance Vader.

"He was fast, all right. I had to kill him."

Red Irons shrugged. "Don't let it bother you, Choc. There's a dozen men in this camp wanted to kill him . . . and not over two or three who stood a chance with him."

So we walked away down the hill. Suddenly, from being just a drifting outlaw, I had become known as a dangerous gunman, a man to reckon with.

Inside, the reaction was hitting me. I was sick, wanted to get off alone, but I had to stand the drinks. There had been no way out for me. I'd had to kill him, but this was the first time I ever needed to kill a man. The first time I ever wanted to kill a man. It scared me.

What would Liza think of me now?

When I put down my glass and turned toward the door, Smoky Hill was there. He looked sort of strange, and right then I knew I was in for it.

"Choc," he said, "Ash Milo wants to see you up on the hill."

EIGHTEEN

When I walked out on that porch I knew I was in trouble. If Mustang Roberts had guessed right and Ash Milo knew me, I was going to have to kill another man. And I would have the problem of getting out with Liza—if she would still go with me after what she had seen.

Standing there on the porch in front of the saloon, I rolled a smoke. Inside I felt empty. I could feel the slow, heavy beating of my heart, and I had a hard time moistening my cigarette, my mouth was that dry.

That walk up the hill, only a hundred and fifty yards or so, was the longest walk I'll ever take.

I felt the sun on my back. I could smell the grass, and off over a distant ridge there was a fluff of white cloud that left a shadow on the salmon cliffs. It might be the last time I'd see that sky or the cliffs.

Gray was down there in the stable. I suddenly wished he was saddled. I was going to need a horse if I came out of this alive.

In my thoughts were the things I had heard. Milo was said to be utterly ruthless, without compassion. He had killed suddenly and without warning. He could be dangerous as a striking rattler, with no need to rattle before he struck.

Liza opened the door. But it was a taller, more lovely Liza.

She would be eighteen now, but there was a quiet maturity in her face that made her look older. There was a great sadness, too.

For a long moment our eyes held, and she searched mine as if she expected to find something there, feared to find it.

"Rye," she said, "I wanted to spare you this. I wanted to." And then she stepped aside and I stepped into the door and I was looking at Ash Milo.

Only I knew him . . . I knew him well. He was the man I had admired most in the world. He was the man I had looked up to and respected. The man who had been my friend when I had no other. He was Logan Pollard.

He was slimmer, older. His hair was mixed with gray, his face was drawn tighter and harder, and his lips had thinned down. Above all, there was in him a tension I did not recall. Always, he had seemed so thoroughly calm, so relaxed, so much in command of himself and all around him.

As though it were yesterday, I remembered the day he interceded for me and stopped McGarry from giving me a whipping. I remembered the day he saved me from the horse thieves when I had walked into a gun battle with them. I remembered the advice he had given me.

He walked toward me, smiling that tight smile, and he held out his hand.

"Rye!" he said. "Rye, it's really you! After all this time!"

There was no hesitation in me. I grabbed his hand and held it hard, and he looked into my eyes and smiled.

"You've made a name for yourself, Rye. And you've stayed on the right side of the law. I'm glad."

"So that's why you kept your outfit away from my town," I said. "You were protecting me."

He smiled, still that tight, quick smile. Only this time there was a hint of cynicism in it, and a little mockery. "No, Rye. I've always known you. I knew if we ever crossed you, we were in real trouble.

"You see, Rye," his voice was almost gentle, "a boy who will

158

fight back when his father is killed is a natural boy. He does what anyone would do, given a chance.

"But you were different. You followed those Indians, and you killed at least one. Moreover, I saw you face McGarry. You weren't afraid. There was iron in you. . . ."

He turned and walked across the room. Liza was looking at me strangely, watching me for something. Me, I was confused, but now I was settling down. I was beginning to think.

"What became of Mary?" I asked.

His back was toward me and for a long time he did not reply, nor did he move. Then he said quietly, "She died in childbirth, Rye. If she'd lived I would probably have stayed right there.

"Remember old Sheriff Balcher? He tried to get me to stay, but I wouldn't listen. I couldn't stay there with those memories, so I left."

Logan Pollard came back to the center of the room. "Sit down, Rye. Please sit down."

It wasn't in me to quibble or to beat around the brush. "Logan," I said, "you know why I'm here?"

The smile left his eyes. He looked at me, taut and watchful. I knew then that all they said of the gunman known as Ash Milo was true. He was a dangerous man . . . and a not entirely sane man.

I'd looked many times into the eyes of dangerous men, and I knew how they looked. But in his eyes there was something else . . . something extra.

"Of course. You've come for Liza. On that score I must disappoint you."

So here it was. Here was the line we drew, the line along which neither of us would yield. Yet I had to try.

"It isn't like you, Logan. You're holding her against her will. That's not your sort of man."

He shrugged, a little irritable frown gathering around his eyes. "Don't be a fool, Rye! She may not wish to stay now, but she'll change. I'm not forcing her into anything, just giving her time to change."

159

"If she were to change at all, Logan, it wouldn't be in this place. No decent woman could live in such a place."

He stood with his feet a little apart, facing me. He was wearing gray-striped trousers and a white shirt with a black string tie. He looked good. He was, I expect, a mighty handsome man. He also wore a gun.

"Rye, you're the man I've needed here. Stay with me. Together we can live like feudal barons. We can have all this!" He waved a hand at the hills. "We can have it to ourselves!"

All this . . . an empire of rock and sand. Someday it would be more, but that was a long way off, and no bunch of outlaws would make it more. Yet this man had helped me. He had been my best friend, and for a long time my only friend. But now I knew I was going to have to leave, and that our friendship was at an end. And I was going to take Liza with me. And it wasn't going to be easy.

"No." I said it flatly. "No, Logan, I'm leaving. And I'm taking Liza with me if she wants to go."

Then I told him about the place back in Maryland. Only I was telling Liza, too. "I'm going to do what you advised, Logan. I'm going to get away from the need for killing before I kill the wrong man, or before I lose all sense of balance and kill too many."

He was very quiet. He rolled a smoke, and then he looked up at me. This was Logan, but it was also the man who had called himself T. J. Farris—the man who had sent for John Lang. The man behind Ben Billings. It was hard to believe how a man could change.

"You can go. Liza stays with me."

"You had Mary," I said quietly. "She was your tie, the person who stood by you, helped you. Liza is the same for me. Liza can be everything to me. We've both known it since we were kids."

"No." He said it as if he didn't want to believe. "No. She stays."

I glanced at Liza. "Will you go with me?"

"Yes, Rye. I will go with you."

"See?" My eyes swung back. "I—"

Logan Pollard was smiling at me. That tight, strange smile, so unlike the warm smile he used to have. He was smiling at me over a gun.

"Rye, I thought I taught you better. Never take your eyes off a man."

"But you're my friend," I said.

His face did not change. He looked a little bored, I thought. Only I'm not always a good judge.

"There are no friends. In this life you take what you want or it's taken from you. You can go now, Rye. You can ride out of the badlands and stay out. I've told the boys to let you go. I told Smoky Hill you were to go after I'd talked with you."

So there it was. He looked at me across a gun the way he had once looked at McGarry, only with that odd difference. He looked at me down the barrel of a gun and I knew he was, with that gun, one of the most dangerous men in the West.

He had taught me other things. Never to draw unless to shoot, never to shoot unless to kill.

The man standing behind that gun was a man who had never drawn but to kill. Rarely in the old days, but now I could see that with the death of Mary, something had happened. The old Logan Pollard was gone.

And here before me in this tight, icy man with the thin-drawn mouth was what I might become. This man who killed wantonly now, who could take a decent girl and hold her until she was finally broken by his will.

And suddenly I knew. I knew that when I turned to go he would kill me.

He would kill me because if I left I would return with armed men to wipe out the Roost. He had admitted I'd been left alone because he'd known how I would react.

"All right," I said. "I'll go. But I wish you'd think it over. We've been friends, and—"

"Stop it!" His tension was mounting. He would have to kill. I knew. "Consider yourself lucky. You did me a favor by killing Chance Vader. Now get out of here. I'm returning the favor by letting you go."

Liza's eyes were wide and frightened. She was trying to warn me, trying to tell me.

I turned, needing the one trick, the thing that would throw him off the one instant I needed, for there is a thing called reaction time, the space of delay between the will and the action.

I started to turn, then suddenly looked back. "Logan," I said, "I've only read Plutarch four times."

"Plutarch?"

He had been set to kill, and the remark threw him off. It took an instant for his mind to react and in that instant I threw myself aside and drew.

It was an action I had practiced when alone, dropping aside and to one knee, the other leg outstretched. And I made the fastest draw of my life. I made it because I had to.

The Smith & Wesson .44 kicked hard against my palm. In the instant I fired I saw his eyes white and ugly and his gun blossom with fire. I was smashed back to the floor, heard the hammer of another bullet drive into the wall back of me, and I fired twice.

Yet even as I fired, I saw the red on his shirt front, and I saw him knocked back and twisted by my shots, so that his third shot went into the ceiling.

Rolling over, I came up fast. He swung his gun and we both shot. He hit me. I felt the numbing shock of the bullet. And then I fired and he fell, tumbling face down, the gun slipping from his hand.

For an instant I stared down at him, holding my gun ready. He turned over and stared up at me, smiling faintly.

"Rye," he said. "Good old Rye. You learned, didn't you?"

His body tightened and twisted, held hard against pain, and then his muscles relaxed.

"Liza," I said, "get a rifle. Stand by the window. We're still in trouble."

He was lying there looking at me. "Think I always knew it, Rye. Think I always knew it would be you. Fate . . . somehow."

He was dying, and he knew it, yet there was still danger in the man, and I could not trust him. He saw it in me, and smiled. "Good boy," he said. "Good boy."

We could hear them coming up the hill. We could hear them all coming. Thirty or more of them, armed and dangerous men.

"I'm going East, Logan. You're the last. I'm going to put my guns away."

My guns were loaded again. He had taught me that. Reload as soon as you stop shooting.

They had stopped outside. I stepped to the door. "Smoky Hill," I said. "You and Bronc. Come on in."

With Liza holding a rifle on the others, they entered one by one.

Logan Pollard looked up at them. He stared at them for a minute, and then looked back at me. "Told you Plutarch would be good reading," he said. "I—"

And he died, just like that. He died there on the floor, and inside I felt sick and empty and lost.

Across his body I looked at them. "His real name was Logan Pollard," I said. "He was my best friend."

Nobody said anything. "I'm going out of here," I said. "She's going with me. I came after her."

Smoky Hill rubbed his hands down his pants. Bronc rolled his quid in his jaws.

"Any argument?" I asked.

"Not any," Bronc said. "You go ahead."

They turned and walked outside and I took Liza by the arm. She held back, just a minute. "You're wounded, Rye!"

"Get what we'll need," I said. "We can't give them time to change their minds."

My side was stiff and sore. I could feel the wetness of blood

163

inside my shirt. But I felt all right. I could make out. I'd have to.

"Rye . . . he was all right to me. He really was."

"I knew him," I said. "He was a good man."

Nobody said anything as we walked out and went down to the stables. Nobody made any argument. Maybe they didn't want to face my guns. Maybe they were too stunned to think about doing anything. Maybe there wasn't anything they wanted to do.

At a seep a dozen miles down the back trail, Liza looked me over. One bullet had cut through the muscle at the top of my shoulder. The second had hit a rib, breaking it and cutting through the flesh and out the back. I'd lost blood.

We met Mustang Roberts and a posse of twenty men coming down Nine Mile Valley, trying to work out the trail. We were riding along together when they saw us, and they just turned around and fell in behind.

And that was the way it was in the old days before the country grew up and men put their guns away.

Someday, and I hope it never comes, there may be a time when the Western hills are empty again and the land will go back to wilderness and the old, hard ways.

Enemies may come into our country and times will have changed, but then the boys will come down from the old high hills and belt on their guns again.

They can do it if they have to. The guns are hung up, the cows roam fat and lazy, but the old spirit is still there, just as it was when the longhorns came up the trail from Texas, and the boys washed the creeks for gold.